C0-AOE-681

Beyond Control

Beyond Control

SEVEN STORIES OF SCIENCE FICTION

edited by

ROBERT SILVERBERG

THOMAS NELSON INC.
Nashville • Camden • New York

Third printing, July 1973

First edition

Library of Congress Cataloging in Publication Data

Silverberg, Robert, comp.
  Beyond control; seven stories of science fiction.

  CONTENTS: Child's play, by W. Tenn.—Autofac, by P.K. Dick.—Adam and no Eve, by A. Bester. [etc.]
  1. Science fiction, American. I. Title.
PZ1.S587Be   813'.0876   72-2897
ISBN 0-8407-6236-4

Acknowledgments

Child's Play, by William Tenn, copyright 1947 by Street & Smith Publications, Inc. Reprinted by permission of the author and Henry Morrison Inc., his agents.

Autofac, by Philip K. Dick, copyright 1955 by Galaxy Publishing Corporation. Reprinted by permission of the author and the author's agents, Scott Meredith Literary Agency, Inc.

Adam and No Eve, by Alfred Bester, copyright 1941 by Street & Smith Publications, Inc. Reprinted by permission of the author.

City of Yesterday, by Terry Carr, copyright © 1967 by Galaxy Publishing Corporation. Reprinted by permission of the author and Henry Morrison Inc., his agents.

The Iron Chancellor, by Robert Silverberg, copyright © 1958 by Galaxy Publishing Corporation. Reprinted by permission of the author and the author's agents, Scott Meredith Literary Agency, Inc.

Contents

Contents

Beyond Control

Introduction

The Greeks, as usual, had a word for it: *hybris*. By that they meant "overweening pride," the blind arrogance that leads men to challenge the gods by reaching beyond the divinely decreed limits of their powers. Inevitably, to commit *hybris* was to invite the vengeance of the angered deities.

But man is by nature a creature who is made restless by boundaries and prohibitions, and is always reaching beyond them; he nibbles the apples of the tree of knowledge, and seeks to expand his kingdom no matter what the gods decree. Thus any aspect of human growth and progress has a certain element of *hybris* in it, and the literature of our world is full of examples of those who pushed their quests for knowledge too far and were struck down by the gods. Science fiction, the special literature of technology, is particularly well supplied with such themes. Again and again, science-fiction stories warn against the terrifying possibilities of disaster that lie hidden in technological progress, and demonstrate the unforeseen and unforeseeable consequences of too boldly seeking to attain the power of a god. Some of the writers of such stories are genuinely frightened by progress, and intend their work as tracts designed to encourage the world to return to simpler times. Others, no enemies of progress, wish only to point out the need for caution and wisdom as we move forward toward the attainment of our scientific goals.

Here are seven stories—some somber, some light-hearted—dealing with the hidden dangers of technological miracles. Like all good science fiction, they are not meant to be read as sermons, but rather were written to entertain and amuse. Like all good science fiction, however, they function on a second level beyond that of diversion; for they are all examinations of the sin of *hybris* and its consequences. They urge us to beware, as we make our way into the glittering future of scientific marvels and wonders—for we are only human and thus capable of error, and in that glittering future there may lie concealed an infinity of perils.

—Robert Silverberg

Child's Play

WILLIAM TENN

"Whatever it is," declares the poet Virgil, "I fear Greeks even when they come bearing gifts." A gift from the future is also something to be feared, evidently—as William Tenn demonstrates in this classic of science fiction.

AFTER THE man from the express company had given the door an untipped slam, Sam Weber decided to move the huge crate under the one light bulb in his room. It was all very well for the messenger to drawl, "I dunno. We don't send 'em; we just deliver 'em, mister"—but there must be some sensible explanation.

With a grunt that began as an anticipatory reflex and ended on a note of surprised annoyance, Sam shoved the box forward the few feet necessary. It was heavy enough; he wondered how the messenger had carried it up the three flights of stairs.

He straightened and frowned down at the garish card which contained his name and address as well as the legend—"Merry Christmas, 2353."

A joke? He didn't know anyone who'd think it funny to send a card dated over four hundred years in the future. Unless one of the comedians in his law school graduating class meant to record his opinion as to when Weber would be trying his first case. Even so—

The letters were shaped strangely, come to think of it, sort of green streaks instead of lines. And the card was a sheet of gold!

Sam decided he was really interested. He ripped the card aside, tore off the flimsy wrapping material—and stopped.

There was no top to the box, no slit in its side, no handle anywhere in sight. It seemed to be a solid, cubical mass of brown stuff. Yet he was positive something had rattled inside when it was moved.

He seized the corners and strained and grunted till it lifted. The underside was as smooth and innocent of openings as the rest. He let it thump back to the floor.

"Ah, well," he said, philosophically, "it's not the gift; it's the principle involved."

Many of his gifts still required appreciative notes. He'd have to work up something special for Aunt Maggie. Her neckties were things of cubistic horror, but he hadn't even sent her a lone handkerchief this Christmas. Every cent had gone into buying that brooch for Tina. Not quite a ring, but maybe she'd consider that under the circumstances—

He turned to walk to his bed which he had drafted into the additional service of desk and chair. He kicked at the great box disconsolately. "Well, if you won't open, you won't open."

As if smarting under the kick, the box opened. A cut appeared on the upper surface, widened rapidly and folded the top back and down on either side like a valise. Sam clapped his forehead and addressed a rapid prayer to every god from Set to Father Divine. Then he remembered what he'd said.

"Close," he suggested.

The box closed, once more as smooth as a baby's bottom.

"Open."

The box opened.

So much for the sideshow, Sam decided. He bent down and peered into the container.

The interior was a crazy mass of shelving on which rested vials filled with blue liquids, jars filled with red solids, transparent tubes showing yellow and green and orange and mauve and other colors which Sam's eyes didn't quite remember. There were seven pieces of intricate apparatus on the bottom which looked as if tube-happy radio hams had assembled them. There was also a book.

Sam picked the book off the bottom and noted numbly that while all its pages were metallic, it was lighter than any paper book he'd ever held.

He carried the book over to the bed and sat down. Then he took a long, deep breath and turned to the first page. *"Gug,"* he said, exhaling his long, deep breath.

In mad, green streaks of letters:

> Bild-a-Man Set #3. This set is intended solely for the use of children between the ages of eleven and thirteen. The equipment, much more advanced than Bild-a-Man Sets 1 and 2, will enable the child of this age-group to build and assemble complete adult humans in perfect working order. The retarded child may also construct the babies and mannikins of the earlier kits. Two disassembleators are provided so that the set can be used again and again with profit. As with Sets 1 and 2, the aid of a Census Keeper in all disassembling is advised. Refills and additional parts may be acquired from The Bild-a-Man Company, 928 Diagonal Level, Glunt City, Ohio. Remember—only with a Bild-a-Man can you build a man!

Weber squeezed his eyes shut. What was that gag in the movie he'd seen last night? Terrific gag. Terrific picture, too. Nice technicolor. Wonder how much the director made a week? The cameraman? Five hundred? A thousand?

He opened his eyes warily. The box was still a squat

cube in the center of his room. The book was still in his shaking hand. And the page read the same.

"Only with a Bild-a-Man can you build a man!" Heaven help a neurotic young lawyer at a time like this!

There was a price list on the next page for "refills and additional parts." Things like one liter of hemoglobin and three grams of assorted enzymes were offered for sale in terms of one slunk fifty and three slunks forty-five. A note on the bottom advertised Set 4: "The thrill of building your first live Martian!"

Fine print announced *pat. pending 2348.*

The third page was a table of contents. Sam gripped the edge of the mattress with one sweating hand and read:

> Chapter I—A child's garden of biochemistry.
> Chapter II—Making simple living things indoors and out.
> Chapter III—Mannikins and what makes them do the world's work.
> Chapter IV—Babies and other small humans.
> Chapter V—Twins for every purpose, twinning yourself and your friends.
> Chapter VI—What you need to build a man.
> Chapter VII—Completing the man.
> Chapter VIII—Disassembling the man.
> Chapter IX—New kinds of life for your leisure moments.

Sam dropped the book back into the box and ran for the mirror. His face was still the same, somewhat like bleached chalk, but fundamentally the same. He hadn't twinned or grown himself a mannikin or devised a new kind of life for his pleasure moments. Everything was snug as a bug in a bughouse.

Very carefully he pushed his eyes back into the proper position in their sockets.

"Dear Aunt Maggie," he began writing feverishly.

"Your ties made the most beautiful gift of my Christmas. My only regret is—"

My only regret is that I have but one life to give for my Christmas present. Who could have gone to such fantastic lengths for a practical joke? Lew Knight? Even Lew must have some reverence in his insensitive body for the institution of Christmas. And Lew didn't have the brains or the patience for a job so involved.

Tina? Tina had the fine talent for complication, all right. But Tina, while possessing a delightful abundance of all other physical attributes, was badly lacking in funnybone.

Sam drew the leather envelope forth and caressed it. Tina's perfume seemed to cling to the surface and move the world back into focus.

The metallic greeting card glinted at him from the floor. Maybe the reverse side contained the sender's name. He picked it up, turned it over.

Nothing but blank gold surface. He was sure of the gold; his father had been a jeweler. The very value of the sheet was rebuttal to the possibility of a practical joke. Besides, again, what was the point?

"Merry Christmas, 2353." Where would humanity be in four hundred years? Traveling to the stars, or beyond—to unimaginable destinations? Using little mannikins to perform the work of machines and robots? Providing children with—

There might be another card or note inside the box. Weber bent down to remove its contents. His eye noted a large grayish jar and the label etched into its surface: *Dehydrated Neurone Preparation, for human construction only.*

He backed away and glared. "Close!"

The thing melted shut. Weber sighed his relief at it and decided to go to bed.

He regretted while undressing that he hadn't thought to

ask the messenger the name of his firm. Knowing the delivery service involved would be useful in tracing the origin of this gruesome gift.

"But then," he repeated as he fell asleep, "it's not the gift—it's the principle! Merry Christmas, me."

The next morning when Lew Knight breezed in with his "Good morning, counselor," Sam waited for the first sly ribbing to start. Lew wasn't the man to hide his humor behind a bushel. But Lew buried his nose in *The New York State Supplement* and kept it there all morning. The other five young lawyers in the communal office appeared either too bored or too busy to have Bild-a-Man sets on their conscience. There were no sly grins, no covert glances, no leading questions.

Tina walked in at ten o'clock, looking like a pinup girl caught with her clothes on.

"Good morning, counselors," she said.

Each in his own way, according to the peculiar gland secretions he was enjoying at the moment, beamed, drooled or nodded a reply. Lew Knight drooled. Sam Weber beamed.

Tina took it all in and analyzed the situation while she fluffed her hair about. Her conclusions evidently involved leaning markedly against Lew Knight's desk and asking what he had for her to do this morning.

Sam bit savagely into Hackleworth *On Torts*. Theoretically, Tina was employed by all seven of them as secretary, switchboard operator and receptionist. Actually, the most faithful performance of her duties entailed nothing more daily than the typing and addressing of two envelopes with an occasional letter to be sealed inside. Once a week there might be a wistful little brief which was never to attain judicial scrutiny. Tina therefore had a fair library of fashion magazines in the first drawer of her desk and a complete cosmetics laboratory in the other two; she spent one third of her working day in the ladies' room swapping stocking prices and sources with other secretaries; she devoted the other two thirds religiously to that one of her employers who as of her arrival seemed to be in the most masculine mood. Her pay was small but her life was full.

Just before lunch, she approached casually with the morning's mail. "Didn't think we'd be too busy this morning, counselor—" she began.

"You thought incorrectly, Miss Hill," he informed her with a brisk irritation that he hoped became him well; "I've been waiting for you to terminate your social engagements so that we could get down to what occasionally passes for business."

She was as startled as an uncushioned kitten. "But—but this isn't Monday. Somerset & Ojack only send you stuff on Mondays."

Sam winced at the reminder that if it weren't for the legal drudgework he received once a week from Somerset & Ojack he would be a lawyer in name only, if not in spirit only. "I have a letter, Miss Hill," he replied steadily. "Whenever you assemble the necessary materials, we can get on with it."

Tina returned in a head-shaking moment with stenographic pad and pencils.

"Regular heading, today's date," Sam began. "Address it to Chamber of Commerce, Glunt City, Ohio. Gentlemen: Would you inform me if you have registered currently with you a firm bearing the name of the Bild-a-Man Company or a firm with any name at all similar? I am also interested in whether a firm bearing the above or related name has recently made known its intention of joining your community. This inquiry is being made informally on behalf of a client who is interested in a product of this organization whose address he has mislaid. Signature and then this P.S.—My client is also curious as to the business possibilities of a street known as

Diagonal Avenue or Diagonal Level. Any data on this address and the organizations presently located there will be greatly appreciated."

Tina batted wide blue eyes at him. "Oh, Sam," she breathed, ignoring the formality he had introduced, "oh, Sam, you have another client. I'm so glad. He looked a little sinister, but in *such* a distinguished manner that I was certain—"

"Who? Who looked a little sinister?"

"Why, your new cli-ent." Sam had the uncomfortable feeling that she had almost added, "stu-pid." "When I came in this morning, there was this terribly tall old man in a long black overcoat talking to the elevator operator. He turned to me—the elevator operator, I mean—and said, 'This is Mr. Weber's secretary. She'll be able to tell you anything you want to know.' Then he sort of winked which I thought was sort of impolite, you know, considering. Then this old man looked at me hard and I felt distinctly uncomfortable and he walked away muttering, 'Either disjointed or predatory personalities. Never normal. Never balanced.' Which I didn't think was very polite, either, I'll have you know, if he *is* your new client!" She sat back and began breathing again.

Tall, sinister old men in long black overcoats pumping the elevator operator about him. Hardly a matter of business. He had no skeletons in his personal closet. Could it be connected with his unusual Christmas present? Sam hummed mentally.

"—but she is my favorite aunt, you know," Tina was saying. "And she came in so unexpectedly."

The girl was explaining about their Christmas date. Sam felt a rush of affection for her as she leaned forward.

"Don't bother," he told her. "I know you couldn't help breaking the date. I was a little sore when you called me, but I got over it; never-hold-a-grudge-against-a-pretty-girl-Sam, I'm known as. How about lunch?"

"Lunch?" She gestured distractedly. "I promised Lew, Mr. Knight, that is—but he wouldn't mind if you came along."

"Fine. Let's go." This would be helping Lew to a spoonful of his own medicine.

Lew Knight took the business of having a crowd instead of a party for lunch as badly as Sam hoped he would. Unfortunately, Lew was able to describe details of his forthcoming case, the probable fees and possible distinction to be reaped thereof. After one or two attempts to bring an interesting will he was rephrasing for Somerset & Ojack into the conversation, Sam subsided into daydreams. Lew immediately dropped *Rosenthal vs. Rosenthal* and leered at Tina conversationally.

Outside the restaurant, snow discolored into slush. Most of the stores were removing Christmas displays. Sam noticed construction sets for children, haloed by tinsel and glittering with artificial snow. Build a radio, a skyscraper, an airplane. But "Only with a Bild-a-Man can you—"

"I'm going home," he announced suddenly. "Something important I just remembered. If anything comes up, call me there."

He was leaving Lew a clear field, he told himself, as he found a seat on the subway. But the bitter truth was that the field was almost as clear when he was around as when he wasn't. Lupine Lew Knight, he had been called in Law School; since the day when he had noticed that Tina had the correct proportions of dress-filling substance, Sam's chances had been worth a crowbar at Fort Knox.

Tina hadn't been wearing his brooch today. Her little finger, right hand, however, had sported an unfamiliar and garish little ring. "Some got it," Sam philosophized. "Some don't got it. I don't got it."

But it would have been nice, with Tina, to have got it.

As he unlocked the door of his room he was surprised by an unmade bed telling with rumpled stoicism of a chambermaid who'd never come. This hadn't happened before—of course! He'd never locked his room before.

The girl must have thought he wanted privacy.

Maybe he had.

Aunt Maggie's ties glittered obscenely at the foot of the bed. He chucked them into the closet as he removed his hat and coat. Then he went over to the washstand and washed his hands, slowly. He turned around.

This was it. At last the great cubical bulk that had been lurking quietly in the corner of his vision was squarely before him. It was there and it undoubtedly contained all the outlandish collection he remembered.

"Open," he said, and the box opened.

The book, still open to the metallic table of contents, was lying at the bottom of the box. Part of it had slipped into the chamber of a strange piece of apparatus. Sam picked both out gingerly.

He slipped the book out and noticed the apparatus consisted mostly of some sort of binoculars, supported by a coil and tube arrangement and bearing on a flat green plate. He turned it over. The underside was lettered in the same streaky way as the book. *Combination Electron Microscope and Workbench.*

Very carefully he placed it on the floor. One by one, he removed the others, from the *Junior Biocalibrator* to the *Jiffy Vitalizer.* Very respectfully he ranged against the box in five multicolored rows the phials of lymph and the jars of basic cartilage. The walls of the chest were lined with indescribably thin and wrinkled sheets; a slight pressure along their edges expanded them into three-dimensional outlines of human organs whose shape and size could be varied with pinching any part of their surface—most indubitably molds.

Quite an assortment. If there was anything solidly scientific to it, that box might mean unimaginable wealth. Or some very useful publicity. Or—well, it should mean something!

If there was anything solidly scientific to it.

Sam flopped down to the bed and opened to *A Child's Garden of Biochemistry*.

At nine that night he squatted next to the Combination Electron Microscope and Workbench and began opening certain small bottles. At nine forty-seven Sam Weber made his first simple living thing.

It wasn't much, if you used the first chapter of Genesis as your standard. Just a primitive brown mold that, in the field of the microscope, fed diffidently on a piece of pretzel, put forth a few spores and died in about twenty minutes. But *he* had made it. He had constructed a specific life-form to feed on the constituents of a specific pretzel; it could survive nowhere else.

He went out to supper with every intention of getting drunk. After just a little alcohol, however, the *deiish* feeling returned and he scurried back to his room.

Never again that evening did he recapture the exultation of the brown mold, though he constructed a giant protein molecule and a whole slew of filterable viruses.

He called the office in the little corner drugstore which was his breakfast nook. "I'll be home all day," he told Tina.

She was a little puzzled. So was Lew Knight, who grabbed the phone. "Hey, counselor, you building up a neighborhood practice? Kid Blackstone is missing out on a lot of cases. Two ambulances have already clanged past the building."

"Yeah," said Sam. "I'll tell him when he comes in."

The weekend was almost upon him, so he decided to take the next day off as well. He wouldn't have any real

work till Monday when the Somerset & Ojack basket
would produce his lone egg.

Before he returned to his room, he purchased a copy of
an advanced bacteriology. It was amusing to construct—
with improvements!—unicellular creatures whose very
place in the scheme of classification was a matter for
argument among scientists of his own day. The Bild-a-
Man manual, of course, merely gave a few examples and
general rules; but with the descriptions in the bacteriology, the world was his oyster.

Which was an idea: he made a few oysters. The shells
weren't hard enough, and he couldn't quite screw his
courage up to the eating point, but they were most unde-
niably bivalves. If he cared to perfect his technique, his
food problem would be solved.

The manual was fairly easy to follow and profusely
illustrated with pictures that expanded into solidity as the
page was opened. Very little was taken for granted; involved explanations followed simpler ones. Only the allu-
sions were occasionally obscure—"This is the principle
used in the phanphophlink toys," "When your teeth are
next yokekkled or demortoned, think of the *Bacterium
cyanogenum* and the humble part it plays," "If you have a
rubicular mannikin around the house, you needn't bother
with the chapter on mannikins."

After a brief search had convinced Sam that whatever
else he now had in his apartment he didn't have a rubicular mannikin, he felt justified in turning to the chapter on
mannikins. He had conquered completely this feeling of
being Pop playing with Junior's toy train: already he had
done more than the world's top biologists ever dreamed of
for the next generation and what might not lie ahead—
what problems might he not yet solve?

"Never forget that mannikins are constructed for one
purpose and one purpose only." I won't, Sam promised.
"Whether they are sanitary mannikins, tailoring manni-

kins, printing mannikins or even sunevviarry mannikins, they are each constructed with one operation of a given process in view. When you make a mannikin that is capable of more than one function, you are committing a crime so serious as to be punishable by public admonition."

"To construct an elementary mannikin—"

It was very difficult. Three times he tore down developing monstrosities and began anew. It wasn't till Sunday afternoon that the mannikin was complete—or rather, incomplete.

Long arms it had—although by an error, one was slightly longer than the other—a faceless head and a trunk. No legs. No eyes or ears, no organs of reproduction. It lay on his bed and gurgled out of the red rim of a mouth that was supposed to serve both for ingress and excretion of food. It waved the long arms, designed for some one simple operation not yet invented, in slow circles.

Sam, watching it, decided that life could be as ugly as an open field latrine in midsummer.

He had to disassemble it. Its length—three feet from almost boneless fingers to tapering, sealed-off trunk—precluded the use of the tiny disassembleator with which he had taken apart the oysters and miscellaneous small creations. There was a bright yellow notice on the large disassembleator, however—"To be used only under the direct supervision of a Census Keeper. Call formula A76 or unstable your id."

"Formula A76" meant about as much as sunevviarry, and Sam decided his id was already sufficiently unstabled, thank you. He'd have to make out without a Census Keeper. The big disassembleator probably used the same general principles as the small one.

He clamped it to a bedpost and adjusted the focus. He snapped the switch set in the smooth underside.

Five minutes later the mannikin was a bright, gooey mess on his bed.

The large disassembleator, Sam was convinced as he tidied his room, did require the supervision of a Census Keeper. Some sort of keeper anyway. He rescued as many of the legless creature's constituents as he could, although he doubted he'd be using the set for the next fifty years or so. He certainly wouldn't ever use the disassembleator again; much less spectacular and disagreeable to shove the whole thing into a meat grinder and crank the handle as it squashed inside.

As he locked the door behind him on his way to a gentle binge, he made a mental note to purchase some fresh sheets the next morning. He'd have to sleep on the floor tonight.

Wrist-deep in Somerset & Ojack minutiae, Sam was conscious of Lew Knight's stares and Tina's puzzled glances. If they only knew, he exulted! But Tina would probably just think it "marr-vell-ouss!" and Lew Knight might make some crack like "Hey! Kid Frankenstein himself!" Come to think of it, though, Lew would probably have worked out some method of duplicating, to a limited extent, the contents of the Bild-a-Man set and marketing it commercially. Whereas he—well, there were other things you could do with the gadget. Plenty of other things.

"Hey, counselor," Lew Knight was perched on the corner of his desk, "what are these long weekends we're taking? You might not make as much money in the law, but does it look right for an associate of mine to sell magazine subscriptions on the side?"

Sam stuffed his ears mentally against the emery-wheel voice. "I've been writing a book."

"A law book? *Weber on Bankruptcy?*"

"No, a juvenile. *Lew Knight, The Neanderthal Nitwit.*"

"Won't sell. The title lacks punch. Something like

Knights, Knaves and Knobheads is what the public goes for these days. By the way, Tina tells me you two had some sort of understanding about New Year's Eve and she doesn't think you'd mind if I took her out instead. I don't think you'd mind either, but I may be prejudiced. Especially since I have a table reservation at Cigale's where there's usually less of a crowd of a New Year's Eve than at the Automat."

"I don't mind."

"Good," said Knight approvingly as he moved away. "By the way, I won that case. Nice juicy fee, too. Thanks for asking."

Tina also wanted to know if he objected to the new arrangements when she brought the mail. Again, he didn't. Where had he been for over two days? He had been busy, very busy. Something entirely new. Something important.

She stared down at him as he separated offers of used cars guaranteed not to have been driven over a quarter of a million miles from caressing reminders that he still owed half the tuition for the last year of law school and when was he going to pay it?

Came a letter that was neither bill nor ad. Sam's heart momentarily lost interest in the monotonous round of pumping that was its lot as he stared at a strange postmark: Glunt City, Ohio.

Dear Sir:

There is no firm in Glunt City at the present time bearing any name similar to "Bild-a-Man Company" nor do we know of any such organization planning to join our little community. We also have no thoroughfare called "Diagonal"; our north-south streets are named after Indian tribes while our east-west avenues are listed numerically in multiples of five.

Glunt City is a restricted residential township; we

intend to keep it that. Only small retailing and service establishments are permitted here. If you are interested in building a home in Glunt City and can furnish proof of white, Christian, Anglo-Saxon ancestry on both sides of your family for fifteen generations, we would be glad to furnish further information.

Thomas H. Plantagenet, Mayor.

P.S. An airfield for privately owned jet and propeller-driven aircraft is being built outside the city limits.

That was sort of that. He would get no refills on any of the vials and bottles even if he had a loose slunk or two with which to pay for the stuff. Better go easy on the material and conserve it as much as possible. But no disassembling!

Would the "Bild-a-Man Company" begin manufacturing at Glunt City some time in the future when it had developed into an industrial metropolis against the constricted wills of its restricted citizenry? Or had his package slid from some different track in the human time stream, some era to be born on an other-dimensional earth? There would have to be a common origin to both, else why the English wordage? And could there be a purpose in his having received it, beneficial—or otherwise?

Tina had been asking a question. Sam detached his mind from shapeless speculation and considered her quite-the-opposite features.

"So if you'd still like me to go out with you New Year's Eve, all I have to do is tell Lew that my mother expects to suffer from her gallstones and I have to stay home. Then I think you could buy the Cigale reservations from him cheap."

"Thanks a lot, Tina, but very honestly I don't have the loose cash right now. You and Lew make a much more logical couple anyhow."

Lew Knight wouldn't have done that. Lew cut throats

with carefree zest. But Tina did seem to go with Lew as a type.

Why? Until Lew had developed a raised eyebrow where Tina was concerned, it had been Sam all the way. The rest of the office had accepted the fact and moved out of their path. It wasn't only a question of Lew's greater success and financial well-being: just that Lew had decided he wanted Tina and had got her.

It hurt. Tina wasn't special; she was no cultural companion, no intellectual equal; but he wanted her. He liked being with her. She was the woman he desired, rightly or wrongly, whether or not there was a sound basis to their relationship. He remembered his parents before a railway accident had orphaned him: they were theoretically incompatible, but they had been terribly happy together.

He was still wondering about it the next night as he flipped the pages of "Twinning yourself and your friends." It would be interesting to twin Tina.

"One for me, one for Lew."

Only the horrible possibility of an error was there. His mannikin had not been perfect: its arms had been of unequal length. Think of a physically lopsided Tina, something he could never bring himself to disassemble, limping extraneously through life.

And then the book warned: "Your constructed twin, though resembling you in every obvious detail, has not had the slow and guarded maturity you have enjoyed. He or she will not be as stable mentally, much less able to cope with unusual situations, much more prone to neurosis. Only a professional carnuplicator, using the finest equipment, can make an exact copy of a human personality. Yours will be able to live and even reproduce, but cannot ever be accepted as a valid and responsible member of society."

Well, he could chance that. A little less stability in Tina would hardly be noticeable; it might be more desirable.

There was a knock. He opened the door, guarding the box from view with his body. His landlady.

"Your door has been locked for the past week, Mr. Weber. That's why the chambermaid hasn't cleaned the room. We thought you didn't want anyone inside."

"Yes." He stepped into the hall and closed the door behind him. "I've been doing some highly important legal work at home."

"Oh." He sensed a murderous curiosity and changed the subject.

"Why all the fine feathers, Mrs. Lipanti—New Year's Eve party?"

She smoothed her frilled black dress self-consciously. "Y-yes. My sister and her husband came in from Springfield today and we were going to make a night of it. Only ... only the girl who was supposed to come over and mind their baby just phoned and said she isn't feeling well. So I guess we won't go unless somebody else, I mean unless we can get someone else to take care ... I mean, somebody who doesn't have a previous engagement and who wouldn't—" Her voice trailed away in assumed embarrassment as she realized the favor was already asked.

Well, after all, he wasn't doing anything tonight. And she had been remarkably pleasant those times when he had to operate on the basis of "Of course I'll have the rest of the rent in a day or so." But why did any one of the earth's two billion humans, when in the possession of an unpleasant buck, pass it automatically to Sam Weber?

Then he remembered Chapter IV on babies and other small humans. Since the night when he had separated the mannikin from its constituent parts, he'd been running through the manual as an intellectual exercise. He didn't feel quite up to making some weird error on a small human. But twinning wasn't supposed to be as difficult.

Only by Gog and by Magog, by Aesculapius the Physician and Kildare the Doctor, he would not disassemble this time. There must be other methods of disposal possible in a large city on a dark night. He'd think of something.

"I'd be glad to watch the baby for a few hours." He started down the hall to anticipate her polite protest. "Don't have a date tonight myself. No, don't mention it, Mrs. Lipanti. Glad to do it."

In the landlady's apartment, her nervous sister briefed him doubtfully. "And that's the only time she cries in a low, steady way so if you move fast there won't be much damage done. Not much, anyway."

He saw them to the door. "I'll be fast enough," he assured the mother. "Just so I get a hint."

Mrs. Lipanti paused at the door. "Did I tell you about the man who was asking after you this afternoon?"

Again? "A sort of tall old man in a long black overcoat?"

"With the most frightening way of staring into your face and talking under his breath. Do you know him?"

"Not exactly. What did he want?"

"Well, he asked if there was a Sam Weaver living here who was a lawyer and had been spending most of his time in his room for the past week. I told him we had a Sam Weber—your first name *is* Sam?—who answered to that description, but that the last Weaver had moved out over a year ago. He just looked at me for a while and said, 'Weaver, Weber—they might have made an error,' and walked out without so much as a good-by or excuse-me. Not what I call a polite gentleman."

Thoughtfully Sam walked back to the child. Strange how sharp a mental picture he had formed of this man! Possibly because the two women who had met him thus far had been very impressionable, although to hear their stories the impression was there to be received.

He doubted there was any mistake: the man had been looking for him on both occasions; his knowledge of

Sam's vacation from foolscap this past week proved that. It did seem as if he weren't interested in meeting him until some moot point of identity should be established beyond the least shadow of a doubt. Something of a legal mind, that.

The whole affair centered around the "Bild-a-Man" set, he was positive. This sulking investigation hadn't started until after the gift from 2353 had been delivered—and Sam had started using it.

But till the character in the long black overcoat paddled up to Sam Weber personally and stated his business, there wasn't very much he could do about it.

Sam went upstairs for his Junior Biocalibrator.

He propped the manual open against the side of the bed and switched the instrument on to full scanning power. The infant gurgled thickly as the calibrator was rolled slowly over its fat body and a section of metal tape unwound from the slot with, according to the manual, a completely detailed physiological description.

It was detailed. Sam gasped as the tape, running through the enlarging viewer, gave information on the child for which a pediatrician would have taken out at least three mortgages on his immortal soul. Thyroid capacity, chromosome quality, cerebral content. All broken down into neat subheads of data for construction purposes. Rate of skull expansion in minutes for the next ten hours; rate of cartilage transformation; changes in hormone secretions while active and at rest.

This was a blueprint; it was like taking canons from a baby.

Sam left the child to a puzzled contemplation of its navel and sped upstairs. With the tape as a guide, he clipped sections of the molds into the required smaller sizes. Then, almost before he knew it consciously, he was constructing a small human.

He was amazed at the ease with which he worked. Skill

was evidently acquired in this game; the mannikin had been much harder to put together. The matter of duplication and working from an informational tape simplified his problems, though.

The child took form under his eyes.

He was finished just an hour and a half after he had taken his first measurements. All except the vitalizing.

A moment's pause, here. The ugly prospect of disassembling stopped him for a moment, but he shook it off. He had to see how well he had done the job. If this child could breathe, what was not possible to him! Besides he couldn't keep it suspended in an inanimate condition very long without running the risk of ruining his work and the materials.

He started the vitalizer.

The child shivered and began a low, steady cry. Sam tore down to the landlady's apartment again and scooped up a square of white linen left on the bed for emergencies. Oh well, some more clean sheets.

After he had made the necessary repairs, he stood back and took a good look at it. He was in a sense a papa. He felt as proud.

It was a perfect little creature, glowing and round with health.

"I have twinned," he said happily.

Every detail correct. The two sides of the face correctly inexact, the duplication of the original child's lunch at the very same point of digestion. Same hair, same eyes—or was it? Sam bent over the infant. He could have sworn the other was a blonde. This child had dark hair which seemed to grow darker as he looked.

He grabbed it with one hand and picked up the Junior Biocalibrator with the other.

Downstairs, he placed the two babies side by side on the big bed. No doubt about it. One was blonde; the other, his plagiarism, was now a definite brunette.

The Biocalibrator showed other differences: Slightly faster pulse for his model. Lower blood count. Minutely higher cerebral capacity, although the content was the same. Adrenalin and bile secretions entirely unalike.

It added up to error. His child might be the superior specimen, or the inferior one, but he had not made a true copy. He had no way of knowing at the moment whether or not the infant he had built could grow into a human maturity. The other could.

Why? He had followed directions faithfully, had consulted the calibrator tape at every step. And this had resulted. Had he waited too long before starting the vitalizer? Or was it just a matter of insufficient skill?

Close to midnight, his watch delicately pointed out. It would be necessary to remove evidences of babymaking before the Sisters Lipanti came home. Sam considered possibilities swiftly.

He came down in a few moments with an old tablecloth and a cardboard carton. He wrapped the child in the tablecloth, vaguely happy that the temperature had risen that night, then placed it in the carton.

The child gurgled at the adventure. Its original on the bed *goo*ed in return. Sam slipped quietly out into the street.

Male and female drunks stumbled along tootling on tiny trumpets. People wished each other a *hic* happy new year as he strode down the necessary three blocks.

As he turned left, he saw the sign: "Urban Foundling Home." There was a light burning over a side door. Convenient, but that was a big city for you.

Sam shrank into the shadow of an alley for a moment as a new idea occurred to him. This had to look genuine. He pulled a pencil out of his breast pocket and scrawled on the side of the carton in as small handwriting as he could manage:

Please take good care of my darling little girl. I am
not married.

Then he deposited the carton on the doorstep and held
his finger on the bell until he heard movement inside. He
was across the street and in the alley again by the time a
nurse had opened the door.

It wasn't until he walked into the boarding house that
he remembered about the navel. He stopped and tried to
recall. No, he had built his little girl without a navel! Her
belly had been perfectly smooth. That's what came of
hurrying! Shoddy workmanship.

There might be a bit of to-do in the foundling home
when they unwrapped the kid. How would they explain it?

Sam slapped his forehead. "Me and Michelangelo. He
adds a navel, I forget one!"

Except for an occasional groan, the office was fairly
quiet the second day of the New Year.

He was going through the last intriguing pages of the
book when he was aware of two people teetering awkwardly near his desk. His eyes left the manual reluctantly:
"New kinds of life for your leisure moments" was really
fascinating!

Tina and Lew Knight.

Sam digested the fact that neither of them was perched
on his desk.

Tina wore the little ring she'd received for Christmas on
the third finger of her left hand; Lew was experimenting
with a sheepish look and finding it difficult.

"Oh, Sam. Last night, Lew . . . Sam, we wanted you to
be the first—Such a surprise, like that, I mean! Why I
almost—Naturally we thought this would be a little difficult . . . Sam, we're going, I mean we expect—"

"—to be married," Lew Knight finished in what was
almost an undertone. For the first time since Sam had

known him he looked uncertain and suspicious of life, like a man who finds a newly hatched octopus in his breakfast orange juice.

"You'd adore the way Lew proposed," Tina was gushing. "So roundabout. And so shy. I told him afterward that I thought for a moment he was talking of something else entirely. I did have trouble understanding you, didn't I, dear?"

"Huh? Oh yeah, you had trouble understanding me." Lew stared at his former rival. "Much of a surprise?"

"Oh, no. No surprise at all. You two fit together so perfectly that I knew it right from the first." Sam mumbled his felicitations, conscious of Tina's searching glances. "And now, if you'll excuse me, there's something I have to take care of immediately. A special sort of wedding present."

Lew was disconcerted. "A wedding present. This early?"

"Why, certainly," Tina told him. "It isn't very easy to get just the right thing. And a special friend like Sam naturally wants to get a very special gift."

Sam decided he had taken enough. He grabbed the manual and his coat and dodged through the door.

By the time he came to the red stone steps of the boarding house, he had reached the conclusion that the wound, while painful, had definitely missed his heart. He was in fact chuckling at the memory of Lew Knight's face when his landlady plucked at his sleeve.

"That man was here again today, Mr. Weber. He said he wanted to see you."

"Which man? The tall, old fellow?"

Mrs. Lipanti nodded, her arms folded complacently across her chest. "Such an unpleasant person! When I told him you weren't in, he insisted I take him up to your room. I said I couldn't do that without your permission and he looked at me fit to kill. I've never believed in the evil eye myself—although I always say where there is smoke there must be fire—but if there is such a thing as an evil eye, he has it."

"Will he be back?"

"Yes. He asked me when you usually return and I said about eight o'clock, figuring that if you didn't want to meet him it would give you time to change your clothes and wash up and leave before he gets here. And, Mr. Weber, if you'll excuse me for saying this, I don't think you want to meet him."

"Thanks. But when he comes in at eight, show him up. If he's the right person, I'm in illegal possession of his property. I want to know where this property originates."

In his room, he put the manual away carefully and told the box to open. The Junior Biocalibrator was not too bulky and newspaper would suffice to cover it. He was on his way uptown in a few minutes with the strangely shaped parcel under his arm.

Did he still want to duplicate Tina, he pondered? Yes, in spite of everything. She was still the woman he desired more than any he had ever known; and with the original married to Lew, the replica would have no choice but himself. Only—the replica would have Tina's characteristics up to the moment the measurements were taken; she might insist on marrying Lew as well.

That would make for a bit of a mad situation. But he was still miles from that bridge. It might even be amusing—

The possibility of error was more annoying. The Tina he would make might be off-center in a number of ways: reds might overlap pinks; like an imperfectly reproduced color photograph she might, in time, come to digest her own stomach; there could very easily be a streak of strange and incurable insanity implicit in his model which would not assert itself until a deep mutual affection had flowered and borne fruit. As yet, he was no great shakes as a twinner and human mimeographer; the errors he had made on Mrs. Lipanti's niece demonstrated his amateur standing.

Sam knew he would never be able to dismantle Tina if she proved defective. Outside of the chivalrous concepts and almost superstitious reverence for womankind pressed into him by a small-town boyhood, there was the unmitigated horror he felt at the idea of such a beloved object going through the same disintegrating process as—well, the mannikin. But if he overlooked an essential in his construction, what other recourse would there be?

Solution: nothing must be overlooked. Sam grinned bitterly as the ancient elevator swayed up to his office. If he only had time for a little more practice with a person whose reactions he knew so exactly that any deviation from the norm would be instantly obvious! But the strange old man would be calling tonight, and, if his business concerned "Bild-a-Man" sets, Sam's experiments might be abruptly curtailed. And where would he find such a person—he had few real friends and no intimate ones. And, to be at all valuable, it would have to be someone he knew as well as himself.

Himself!

"Floor, sir." The elevator operator was looking at him reproachfully. Sam's exultant shout had caused him to bring the carrier to a spasmodic stop six inches under the floor level, something he had not done since that bygone day when he had first nervously reached for the controls. He felt his craftmanship was under a shadow as he morosely closed the door behind the lawyer.

And why not himself? He knew his own physical attributes better than he knew Tina's; any mental instability on the part of his reproduced self would be readily discernible long before it reached the point of psychosis or worse. And the beauty of it was that he would have no compunc-

tion in dissembling a superfluous Sam Weber. Quite the contrary: the horror in that situation would be the continued existence of a duplicate personality; its removal would be a relief.

Twinning himself would provide the necessary practice in a familiar medium. Ideal. He'd have to take careful notes so that if anything went wrong he'd know just where to avoid going off the track in making his own personal Tina.

And maybe the old geezer wasn't interested in the set at all. Even if he was, Sam could take his landlady's advice and not be at home when he called. Silver linings wherever he looked.

Lew Knight stared at the instrument in Sam's hands. "What in the sacred name of Blackstone and all his commentaries is that? Looks like a lawn mower for a window box!"

"It's uh, sort of a measuring gadget. Gives the right size for one thing and another and this and that. Won't be able to get you the wedding present I have in mind unless I know the right size. Or sizes. Tina, would you mind stepping out into the hall?"

"Nooo." She looked dubiously at the gadget. "It won't hurt?"

It wouldn't hurt a bit, Sam assured her. "I just want to keep this a secret from Lew till after the ceremony."

She brightened at that and preceded Sam through the door. "Hey, counselor," one of the other young lawyers called at Lew as they left. "Hey, counselor, don't let him do that. Possession is nine points, Sam always says. He'll never bring her back."

Lew chuckled weakly and bent over his work.

"Now I want you to go into the ladies' room," Sam explained to a bewildered Tina. "I'll stand guard outside and tell the other customers that the place is out of order.

If another woman is inside wait until she leaves. Then strip."

"Strip?" Tina squealed.

He nodded. Then very carefully, emphasizing every significant detail of operation, he told her how to use the Junior Biocalibrator. How she must be careful to kick the switch and set the tape running. How she must cover every external square inch of her body. "This little arm will enable you to lower it down your back. No questions now. Git."

She was back in fifteen minutes, fluffing her dress into place and studying the tape with a rapt frown. "This is the *strangest* thing—According to the spool, my iodine content—"

Sam snaffled the Biocalibrator hurriedly. "Don't give it another thought. It's a code, kind of. Tells me just what size and how many of what kind. You'll be crazy about the gift when you see it."

"I know I will." She bent over him as he kneeled and examined the tape to make certain she had applied the instrument correctly. "You know, Sam, I always felt your taste was perfect. I want you to come and visit us often after we're married. You can have such beautiful ideas! Lew is a bit too ... too businesslike, isn't he? I mean it's necessary for success and all that, but success isn't everything. I mean you have to have culture, too. You'll help me keep cultured, won't you, Sam?"

"Sure," Sam said vaguely. The tape was complete. Now to get started! "Anything I can do—glad to help."

He rang for the elevator and noticed the forlorn uncertainty with which she watched him. "Don't worry, Tina. You and Lew will be very happy together. And you'll love this wedding present." But not as much as I will, he told himself as he stepped into the elevator.

Back in his room, he emptied the machine and undressed. In a few moments he had another tape on himself. He would have liked to consider it for a while, but being this close to the goal made him impatient. He locked the door, cleaned his room hurriedly of accumulated junk—remembering to grunt in annoyance at Aunt Maggie's ties: the blue and red one almost lighted up the room—ordered the box to open—and he was ready to begin.

First the water. With the huge amount of water necessary to the human body, especially in the case of an adult, he might as well start collecting it now. He had bought several pans and it would take his lone faucet some time to fill them all.

As he placed the first pot under the tap, Sam wondered suddenly if its chemical impurities might affect the end product. Of course it might! These children of 2353 would probably take absolutely pure H_2O as a matter of daily use; the manual hadn't mentioned the subject, but how did he know what kind of water they had available? Well, he'd boil this batch over his chemical stove; when he got to making Tina he could see about getting *aqua* completely *pura*.

Score another point for making a simulacrum of Sam first.

While waiting for the water to boil, he arranged his supplies to positions of maximum availability. They were getting low. That baby had taken up quite a bit of useful ingredients; too bad he hadn't seen his way clear to disassembling it. That meant if there were any argument in favor of allowing the replica of himself to go on living, it was now invalid. He'd have to take it apart in order to have enough for Tina II. (Or Tina prime?)

He leafed through Chapters VI, VII and VIII on the ingredients, completion and disassembling of a man. He'd been through this several times before; but he'd passed more than one law exam on the strength of a last-minute review.

The constant reference to mental instability disturbed him. "The humans constructed with this set will, at the very best, show most of the superstitious tendencies, and neurosis-compulsions of medieval mankind. In the long run they are not normal; take great care not to consider them such." Well, it wouldn't make too much difference in Tina's case—and that was all that was important.

When he had finished adjusting the molds to the correct sizes, he fastened the vitalizer to the bed. Then—very, very slowly and with repeated glances at the manual, he began to duplicate Sam Weber. He learned more of his physical limitations and capabilities in the next two hours than any man had ever known since the day when an inconspicuous primate had investigated the possibilities of ground locomotion upon the nether extremities alone.

Strangely enough, he felt neither awe nor exultation. It was like building a radio receiver for the first time. Child's play.

Most of the vials and jars were empty when he had finished. The damp molds were stacked inside the box, still in their three-dimensional outline. The manual lay neglected on the floor.

Sam Weber stood near the bed looking down at Sam Weber on the bed.

All that remained was vitalizing. He daren't wait too long or imperfections might set in and the errors of the baby be repeated. He shook off a nauseating feeling of unreality, made certain that the big disassembleator was within reach and set the Jiffy Vitalizer in motion.

The man on the bed coughed. He stirred. He sat up.

"Wow!" he said. "Pretty good, if I do say so myself!" And then he had leaped off the bed and seized the disassembleator. He tore great chunks of wiring out of the center, threw it to the floor and kicked it into shapelessness. "No Sword of Damocles going to hang over *my* head," he informed an open-mouthed Sam Weber. "Although, I could have used it on you, come to think of it."

Sam eased himself to the mattress and sat down. His mind stopped rearing and whinnied to a halt. He had been so impressed with the helplessness of the baby and the mannikin that he had never dreamed of the possibility that his duplicate would enter upon life with such enthusiasm. He should have, though; this was a full-grown man, created at a moment of complete physical and mental activity.

"This is bad," he said at last in a hoarse voice. "You're unstable. You can't be admitted into normal society."

"I'm unstable?" his image asked. "Look who's talking! The guy who's been mooning his way through his adult life, who wants to marry an overdressed, conceited collection of biological impulses that would come crawling on her knees to any man sensible enough to push the right buttons—"

"You leave Tina's name out of this," Sam told him, feeling acutely uncomfortable at the theatrical phrase.

His double looked at him and grinned. "O.K., I will. But not her body! Now, look here, Sam or Weber or whatever you want me to call you, you can live your life and I'll live mine. I won't even be a lawyer if that'll make you happy. But as far as Tina is concerned, now that there are no ingredients to make a copy—that was a rotten escapist idea, by the way—I have enough of your likes and dislikes to want her badly. And I can have her, whereas you can't. You don't have the gumption."

Sam leaped to his feet and doubled his fists. Then he saw the other's entirely equal size and slightly more assured twinkle. There was no point in fighting—that would end in a draw, at best. He went back to reason.

"According to the manual," he began, "you are prone to neurosis—"

"The manual! The manual was written for children of four centuries hence, with quite a bit of selective breeding and scientific education behind them. Personally, I think I'm a—"

There was a double knock on the door. "Mr. Weber."

"Yes," they both said simultaneously.

Outside, the landlady gasped and began speaking in an uncertain voice. "Th-that gentleman is downstairs. He'd like to see you. Shall I tell him you're in?"

"No, I'm not at home," said the double.

"Tell him I left an hour ago," said Sam at exactly the same moment.

There was another, longer gasp and the sound of footsteps receding hurriedly.

"That's one clever way to handle a situation," Sam's facsimile exploded. "Couldn't you keep your mouth shut? The poor woman's probably gone off to have a fit."

"You forget that this is my room and you are just an experiment that went wrong," Sam told him hotly. "I have just as much right, in fact more right . . . hey, what do you think you're doing?"

The other had thrown open the closet door and was stepping into a pair of pants. "Just getting dressed. You can wander around in the nude if you find it exciting, but I want to look a bit respectable."

"I undressed to take my measurements . . . or your measurements. Those are my clothes, this is my room—"

"Look, take it easy. You could never prove it in a court of law. Don't make me go into that cliché about what's yours is mine and so forth."

Heavy feet resounded through the hall. They stopped outside the room. Cymbals seemed to clash all around them and there was a panic-stricken sense of unendurable heat. Then shrill echoes fled into the distance. The walls stopped shuddering.

Silence and a smell of burning wood.

They whirled in time to see a terribly tall, terribly old man in a long black overcoat walking through the smoldering remains of the door. Much too tall for the entrance, he did not stoop as he came in; rather, he drew his head down into his garment and shot it up again. Instinctively, they moved close together.

His eyes, all shiny black iris without any whites, were set back deep in the shadow of his head. They reminded Sam Weber of the scanners on the Biocalibrator: they tabulated, deduced, rather than saw.

"I was afraid I would be too late," he rumbled at last in weird, clipped tones. "You have already duplicated yourself, Mr. Weber, making necessary unpleasant rearrangements. And the duplicate has destroyed the disassembleator. Too bad. I shall have to do it manually. An ugly job."

He came further into the room until they could almost breathe their fright upon him. "This affair has already dislocated four major programs, but we had to move in accepted cultural grooves and be absolutely certain of the recipient's identity before we could act to withdraw the set. Mrs. Lipanti's collapse naturally stimulated emergency measures."

The duplicate cleared his throat. "You are—"

"Not exactly human. A humble civil servant of precision manufacture. I am Census Keeper for the entire twenty-ninth oblong. You see, your set was intended for the Thregander children, who are on a field trip in this oblong. One of the Threganders who has a Weber chart requested the set through the chrondromos which, in an attempt at the supernormal, unstabled without carnuplicating. You therefore received the package instead. Unfortunately, the unstabling was so complete that we were forced to locate you by indirect methods."

The Census Keeper paused and Sam's double hitched his pants nervously. Sam wished he had anything—even a fig leaf—to cover his nakedness. He felt like a character in the Garden of Eden trying to build up a logical case for apple-eating. He appreciated glumly how much more than "Bild-a-Man" sets clothes had to do with the making of a man.

"We will have to recover the set, of course," the staccato thunder continued, "and readjust any discrepancies it has caused. Once the matter has been cleared up, however, your life will be allowed to resume its normal progression. Meanwhile, the problem is which of you is the original Sam Weber?"

"I am," they both quavered—and turned to glare at each other.

"Difficulties," the old man rumbled. He sighed like an arctic wind. "I always have difficulties! Why can't I ever have a simple case like a carnuplicator?"

"Look here," the duplicate began. "The original will be—"

"Less unstable and of better emotional balance than the replica," Sam interrupted. "Now, it seems—"

"That you should be able to tell the difference," the other concluded breathlessly. "From what you see and have seen of us, can't you decide which is the more valid member of society?"

What a pathetic confidence, Sam thought, the fellow was trying to display! Didn't he know he was up against someone who could really discern mental differences? This was no fumbling psychiatrist of the present; here was a creature who could see through externals to the most coherent personality beneath.

"I can, naturally. Now, just a moment." He studied them carefully, his eyes traveling with judicious leisure up and down their bodies. They waited, fidgeting, in a silence that pounded.

"Yes," the old man said at last. "Yes. Quite."

He walked forward.

A long, thin arm shot out.

He started to disassemble Sam Weber.

"But listennnnn—" began Weber in a yell that turned into a high scream and died in a liquid mumble.

"It would be better for your sanity if you didn't watch," the Census Keeper suggested.

The duplicate exhaled slowly, turned away and began to button a shirt. Behind him the mumbling continued, rising and falling in pitch.

"You see," came the clipped, rumbling accents, "it's not the gift we're afraid of letting you have—it's the principle involved. Your civilization isn't ready for it. You understand."

"Perfectly," replied the counterfeit Weber, knotting Aunt Maggie's blue-and-red tie.

Autofac

PHILIP K. DICK

Everyone knows the old tale of the sorcerer's apprentice—who knew the spell that made the broom carry water from the well, but who didn't know the spell that would get the broom to stop fetching water when the house was flooded. In a way, twentieth-century industrial society is reliving the woes of the sorcerer's apprentice: we have conjured up a mighty technological civilization, which now marches on seemingly unchecked and uncheckable, devouring our planet while we hunt in vain for the spell that will get things under control. In this grim story, Philip K. Dick, one of science fiction's unquestioned masters, vividly portrays the ultimate extension of this process.

TENSION hung over the three waiting men. They smoked, paced back and forth, kicked aimlessly at weeds growing by the side of the road. A hot noonday sun glared down on brown fields, rows of neat plastic houses, the distant line of mountains to the west.

"Almost time," Earl Perine said, knotting his skinny hands together. "It varies according to the load, a half-second for every additional pound."

Bitterly, Morrison answered. "You've got it plotted? You're as bad as it is. Let's pretend it just *happens* to be late."

The third man said nothing. O'Neill was visiting from another settlement; he didn't know Perine and Morrison well enough to argue with them. Instead, he crouched down and arranged the papers clipped to his aluminum checkboard. In the blazing sun, O'Neill's arms were tanned, furry, glistening with sweat. Wiry, with tangled gray hair, horn-rimmed glasses, he was older than the other two. He wore slacks, a sports shirt and crepe-soled shoes. Between his fingers, his fountain pen glittered, metallic and efficient.

"What're you writing?" Perine grumbled.

"I'm laying out the procedure we're going to employ," O'Neill said mildly. "Better to systemize it now, instead of trying at random. We want to know what we tried and what didn't work. Otherwise we'll go around in a circle. The problem we have here is one of communication; that's how I see it."

"Communication," Morrison agreed in his deep, chesty voice. "Yes, we can't get in touch with the damn thing. It comes, leaves off its load and goes on—there's no contact between us and it."

"It's a machine," Perine said excitedly. "It's dead—blind and deaf."

"But it's in contact with the outside world," O'Neill pointed out. "There has to be some way to get to it. Specific semantic signals are meaningful to it; all we have to do is find those signals. Rediscover, actually. Maybe half a dozen out of a billion possibilities."

A low rumble interrupted the three men. They glanced up, wary and alert. The time had come.

"Here it is," Perine said. "Okay, wise guy, let's see you make one single change in its routine."

The truck was massive, rumbling under its tightly packed load. In many ways, it resembled conventional human-operated transportation vehicles, but with one exception—there was no driver's cabin. The horizontal surface was a loading stage, and the part that would normally be the headlights and radiator grill was a fibrous, spongelike mass of receptors, the limited sensory apparatus of this mobile utility extension.

Aware of the three men, the truck slowed to a halt,
shifted gears and pulled on its emergency brake. A moment passed as relays moved into action; then a portion
of the loading surface tilted and a cascade of heavy cartons spilled down onto the brown dust of the roadway.
With the objects fluttered a detailed inventory sheet.

"You know what to do," O'Neill said rapidly. "Hurry
up, before it gets out of here."

Expertly, grimly, the three men grabbed up the deposited cartons and ripped the protective wrappers from
them. Objects gleamed: a binocular microscope, a portable radio, heaps of plastic dishes, medical supplies, razor
blades, clothing, food. Most of the shipment, as usual,
was food. The three men systematically began smashing
the objects. In a few minutes, there was nothing but a
chaos of debris littered around them.

"That's that," O'Neill panted, stepping back. He fumbled for his checksheet. "Now let's see what it does."

The truck had begun to move away; abruptly it stopped
and backed toward them. Its receptors had taken in the
fact that the three men had demolished the dropped-off
portion of the load. It spun in a grinding half-circle and
came around to face its receptor bank in their direction.
Up went its antenna; it had begun communicating with
the factory. Instructions were on the way.

A second, identical load was tilted and shoved off the
truck.

"We failed," Perine groaned as a duplicate inventory
sheet fluttered after the new load. "We destroyed all that
stuff for nothing."

"What now?" Morrison asked O'Neill. "What's the
next stratagem on your board?"

"Give me a hand." O'Neill grabbed up a carton and
lugged it back to the truck. Sliding the carton onto the
platform, he turned for another. The other two men

followed clumsily after him. They put the load back onto the truck. As the truck started forward, the last square box was again in place.

The truck hesitated. Its receptors registered the return of its load. From within its works came a low, sustained buzzing.

"This may drive it crazy," O'Neill commented, sweating. "It went through its operation and accomplished nothing."

The truck made a short, abortive move toward going on. Then it swung purposefully around and, in a blur of speed, again dumped the load onto the road.

"Get them!" O'Neill yelled. The three men grabbed up the cartons and feverishly reloaded them. But as fast as the cartons were shoved back on the horizontal stage, the truck's grapples tilted them down its far-side ramps and onto the road.

"No use," Morrison said, breathing hard. "Water through a sieve."

"We're licked," Perine gasped in wretched agreement, "like always. We humans lose every time."

The truck regarded them calmly, its receptors blank and impassive. It was doing its job. The planetwide network of automatic factories was smoothly performing the task imposed on it five years before, in the early days of the Total Global Conflict.

"There it goes," Morrison observed dismally. The truck's antenna had come down; it shifted into low gear and released its parking brake.

"One last try," O'Neill said. He swept up one of the cartons and ripped it open. From it he dragged a ten-gallon milk tank and unscrewed the lid. "Silly as it seems."

"This is absurd," Perine protested. Reluctantly, he found a cup among the littered debris and dipped it into the milk. "A kid's game!"

The truck had paused to observe them.

"Do it," O'Neill ordered sharply. "Exactly the way we practiced it."

The three of them drank quickly from the milk tank, visibly allowing the milk to spill down their chins; there had to be no mistaking what they were doing.

As planned, O'Neill was the first. His face twisting in revulsion, he hurled the cup away and violently spat milk into the road.

"God's sake!" he choked.

The other two did the same; stamping and loudly cursing, they kicked over the milk tank and glared accusingly at the truck.

"It's no good!" Morrison roared.

Curious, the truck came slowly back. Electronic synapses clicked and whirred, responding to the situation; its antenna shot up like a flagpole.

"I think this is it," O'Neill said, trembling. As the truck watched, he dragged out a second milk tank, unscrewed its lid and tasted the contents. "The same!" he shouted at the truck. "It's just as bad!"

From the truck popped a metal cylinder. The cylinder dropped at Morrison's feet; he quickly snatched it up and tore it open.

STATE NATURE OF DEFECT

The instruction sheets listed rows of possible defects, with neat boxes by each; a punch-stick was included to indicate the particular deficiency of the product.

"What'll I check?" Morrison asked. "Contaminated? Bacterial? Sour? Rancid? Incorrectly labeled? Broken? Crushed? Cracked? Bent? Soiled?"

Thinking rapidly, O'Neill said, "Don't check any of

them. The factory's undoubtedly ready to test and resample. It'll make its own analysis and then ignore us." His face glowed as frantic inspiration came. "Write in that blank at the bottom. It's an open space for further data."

"Write what?"

O'Neill said, "Write: *the product is thoroughly pizzled.*"

"What's that?" Perine demanded, baffled.

"Write it! It's a semantic garble—the factory won't be able to understand it. Maybe we can jam the works."

With O'Neill's pen, Morrison carefully wrote that the milk was pizzled. Shaking his head, he resealed the cylinder and returned it to the truck. The truck swept up the milk tanks and slammed its railing tidily into place. With a shriek of tires, it hurtled off. From its slot, a final cylinder bounced; the truck hurriedly departed, leaving the cylinder lying in the dust.

O'Neill got it open and held up the paper for the others to see.

A FACTORY REPRESENTATIVE WILL BE SENT OUT. BE PREPARED TO SUPPLY COMPLETE DATA ON PRODUCT DEFICIENCY.

For a moment, the three men were silent. Then Perine began to giggle. "We did it. We contacted it. We got across."

"We sure did," O'Neill agreed. "It never heard of a product being pizzled."

Cut into the base of the mountains lay the vast metallic cube of the Kansas City factory. Its surface was corroded, pitted with radiation pox, cracked and scarred from the five years of war that had swept over it. Most of the factory was buried subsurface, only its entrance stages visible. The truck was a speck rumbling at high speed toward the expanse of black metal. Presently an opening formed in the uniform surface; the truck plunged into it and disappeared inside. The entrance snapped shut.

"Now the big job remains," O'Neill said. "Now we have to persuade it to close down operations—to shut itself off."

II

Judith O'Neill served hot black coffee to the people sitting around the living room. Her husband talked while the others listened. O'Neill was as close to being an authority on the autofac system as could still be found.

In his own area, the Chicago region, he had shorted out the protective fence of the local factory long enough to get away with the data tapes stored in its posterior brain. The factory, of course, had immediately reconstructed a better type of fence. But he had shown that the factories were not infallible.

"The Institute of Applied Cybernetics," O'Neill explained, "had complete control over the network. Blame the war. Blame the big noise along the lines of communication that wiped out the knowledge we need. In any case, the Institute failed to transmit its information to us, so we can't transmit our information to the factories—the news that the war is over and we're ready to resume control of industrial operations."

"And meanwhile," Morrison added sourly, "the damn network expands and consumes more of our natural resources all the time."

"I get the feeling," Judith said, "that if I stamped hard enough, I'd fall right down into a factory tunnel. They must have mines everywhere by now."

"Isn't there some limiting injunction?" Perine asked nervously. "Were they set up to expand indefinitely?"

"Each factory is limited to its own operational area," O'Neill said, "but the network itself is unbounded. It can go on scooping up our resources forever. The Institute decided it gets top priority; we mere people come second."

"Will there be *anything* left for us?" Morrison wanted to know.

"Not unless we can stop the network's operations. It's already used up half a dozen basic minerals. Its search teams are out all the time, from every factory, looking everywhere for some last scrap to drag home."

"What would happen if tunnels from two factories crossed each other?"

O'Neill shrugged. "Normally, that won't happen. Each factory has its own special section of our planet, its own private cut of the pie for its exclusive use."

"But it *could* happen."

"Well, they're raw-material-tropic; as long as there's anything left, they'll hunt it down." O'Neill pondered the idea with growing interest. "It's something to consider. I suppose as things get scarcer—"

He stopped talking. A figure had come into the room; it stood silently by the door, surveying them all.

In the dull shadows, the figure looked almost human. For a brief moment, O'Neill thought it was a settlement latecomer. Then, as it moved forward, he realized that it was only quasi-human: a functional upright biped chassis, with data-receptors mounted at the top, effectors and proprioceptors mounted in a downward worm that ended in floor-grippers. Its resemblance to a human being was testimony to nature's efficiency; no sentimental imitation was intended.

The factory representative had arrived.

It began without preamble. "This is a data-collecting machine capable of communicating on an oral basis. It contains both broadcasting and receiving apparatus and can integrate facts relevant to its line of inquiry." The voice was pleasant, confident. Obviously it was a tape, recorded by some Institute technician before the war. Coming from the quasi-human shape, it sounded grotesque; O'Neill could vividly imagine the dead young man whose cheerful voice now issued from the mechanical mouth of this upright construction of steel and wiring.

"One word of caution," the pleasant voice continued. "It is fruitless to consider this receptor human and to engage it in discussions for which it is not equipped. Although purposeful, it is not capable of conceptual thought; it can only reassemble material already available to it."

The optimistic voice clicked out and a second voice came on. It resembled the first, but now there were no intonations or personal mannerisms. The machine was utilizing the dead man's phonetic speech-pattern for its own communication.

"Analysis of the rejected product," it stated, "shows no foreign elements or noticeable deterioration. The product meets the continual testing-standards employed throughout the network. Rejection is therefore on a basis outside the test area; standards not available to the network are being employed."

"That's right," O'Neill agreed. Weighing his words with care, he continued, "We found the milk substandard. We want nothing to do with it. We insist on more careful output."

The machine responded presently. "The semantic content of the term *pizzled* is unfamiliar to the network. It does not exist in the taped vocabulary. Can you present a factual analysis of the milk in terms of specific elements present or absent?"

"No," O'Neill said warily; the game he was playing was intricate and dangerous. "Pizzled is an over-all term. It can't be reduced to chemical constituents."

"What does pizzled signify?" the machine asked. "Can you define it in terms of alternate semantic symbols?"

O'Neill hesitated. The representative had to be steered from its special inquiry to more general regions, to the ultimate problem of closing down the network. If he could pry it open at any point, get the theoretical discussion started . . .

"Pizzled," he stated, "means the condition of a product that is manufactured when no need exists. It indicates the rejection of objects on the grounds that they are no longer wanted."

The representative said, "Network analysis shows a need of high-grade pasteurized milk-substitute in this area. There is no alternate source; the network controls all the synthetic mammary-type equipment in existence." It added, "Original taped instructions describe milk as an essential to human diet."

O'Neill was being outwitted; the machine was returning the discussion to the specific. "We've decided," he said desperately, "that we don't *want* any more milk. We'd prefer to go without it, at least until we can locate cows."

"That is contrary to the network tapes," the representative objected. "There are no cows. All milk is produced synthetically."

"Then we'll produce it synthetically ourselves," Morrison broke in impatiently. "Why can't we take over the machines? My God, we're not children! We can run our own lives!"

The factory representative moved toward the door. "Until such time as your community finds other sources of milk supply, the network will continue to supply you. Analytical and evaluating apparatus will remain in this area, conducting the customary random sampling."

Perine shouted futilely, "How can we find other sources? You have the whole setup! You're running the whole show!" Following after it, he bellowed, "You say we're not ready to run things—you claim we're not capable. How do you know? You don't give us a chance! We'll never have a chance!"

O'Neill was petrified. The machine was leaving; its one-track mind had completely triumphed.

"Look," he said hoarsely, blocking its way. "We want you to shut down, understand. We want to take over your equipment and run it ourselves. The war's over with. Damn it, you're not needed any more!"

The factory representative paused briefly at the door. "The inoperative cycle," it said, "is not geared to begin until network production merely duplicates outside production. There is at this time, according to our continual sampling, no outside production. Therefore network production continues."

Without warning, Morrison swung the steel pipe in his hand. It slashed against the machine's shoulder and burst through the elaborate network of sensory apparatus that made up its chest. The tank of receptors shattered; bits of glass, wiring and minute parts showered everywhere.

"It's a paradox!" Morrison yelled. "A word game—a semantic game they're pulling on us. The Cyberneticists have it rigged." He raised the pipe and again brought it down savagely on the unprotesting machine. "They've got us hamstrung. We're completely helpless."

The room was in uproar. "It's the only way," Perine gasped as he pushed past O'Neill. "We'll have to destroy them—it's the network or us." Grabbing down a lamp, he hurled it in the "face" of the factory representative. The lamp and the intricate surface of plastic burst; Perine waded in, groping blindly for the machine. Now all the people in the room were closing furiously around the upright cylinder, their impotent resentment boiling over.

The machine sank down and disappeared as they dragged it to the floor.

Trembling, O'Neill turned away. His wife caught hold of his arm and led him to the side of the room.

"The idiots," he said dejectedly. "They can't destroy it; they'll only teach it to build more defenses. They're making the whole problem worse."

Into the living room rolled a network repair team. Expertly, the mechanical units detached themselves from the half-track mother-bug and scurried toward the mound of struggling humans. They slid between people and rapidly burrowed. A moment later, the inert carcass of the factory representative was dragged into the hopper of the mother-bug. Parts were collected, torn remnants gathered up and carried off. The last plastic strut and gear was located. Then the units restationed themselves on the bug and the team departed.

Through the open door came a second factory representative, an exact duplicate of the first. And outside in the hall stood two more upright machines. The settlement had been combed at random by a corps of representatives. Like a horde of ants, the mobile data-collecting machines had filtered through the town until, by chance, one of them had come across O'Neill.

"Destruction of network mobile data-gathering equipment is detrimental to best human interests," the factory representative informed the roomful of people. "Raw material intake is at a dangerously low ebb; what basic materials still exist should be utilized in the manufacture of consumer commodities."

O'Neill and the machine stood facing each other.

"Oh?" O'Neill said softly. "That's interesting. I wonder what you're lowest on—and what you'd really be willing to fight for."

Helicopter rotors whined tinnily above O'Neill's head;

he ignored them and peered through the cabin window at the ground not far below.

Slag and ruins stretched everywhere. Weeds poked their way up, sickly stalks among which insects scuttled. Here and there, rat colonies were visible: matted hovels constructed of bone and rubble. Radiation had mutated the rats, along with most insects and animals. A little farther, O'Neill identified a squadron of birds pursuing a ground squirrel. The squirrel dived into a carefully prepared crack in the surface of slag and the birds turned, thwarted.

"You think we'll ever have it rebuilt?" Morrison asked. "It makes me sick to look at it."

"In time," O'Neill answered. "Assuming, of course, that we get industrial control back. And assuming that anything remains to work with. At best, it'll be slow. We'll have to inch out from the settlements."

To the right was a human colony, tattered scarecrows, gaunt and emaciated, living among the ruins of what had once been a town. A few acres of barren soil had been cleared; drooping vegetables wilted in the sun, chickens wandered listlessly here and there, and a fly-bothered horse lay panting in the shade of a crude shed.

"Ruins-squatters," O'Neill said gloomily. "Too far from the network—not tangent to any of the factories."

"It's their own fault," Morrison told him angrily. "They could come into one of the settlements."

"That was their town. They're trying to do what *we're* trying to do—build up things again on their own. But they're starting now, without tools or machines, with their bare hands, nailing together bits of rubble. And it won't work. We need machines. We can't repair ruins; we've got to start industrial production."

Ahead lay a series of broken hills, chipped remains that had once been a ridge. Beyond stretched out the titanic ugly sore of an H-bomb crater, half filled with stagnant water and slime, a disease-ridden inland sea.

And beyond that—a glitter of busy motion.

"There," O'Neill said tensely. He lowered the helicopter rapidly. "Can you tell which factory they're from?"

"They all look alike to me," Morrison muttered, leaning over to see. "We'll have to wait and follow them back, when they get a load."

"*If* they get a load," O'Neill corrected.

The autofac exploring crew ignored the helicopter buzzing overhead and concentrated on its job. Ahead of the main truck scuttled two tractors; they made their way up mounds of rubble, probes burgeoning like quills, shot down the far slope and disappeared into a blanket of ash that lay spread over the slag. The two scouts burrowed until only their antennas were visible. They burst up to the surface and scuttled on, their treads whirring and clanking.

"What are they after?" Morrison asked.

"God knows." O'Neill leafed intently through the papers on his clipboard. "We'll have to analyze all our back-order slips."

Below them, the autofac exploring crew disappeared behind. The helicopter passed over a deserted stretch of sand and slag on which nothing moved. A grove of scrub-brush appeared and then, far to the right, a series of tiny moving dots.

A procession of automatic ore carts was racing over the bleak slag, a string of rapidly moving metal trucks that followed one another nose to tail. O'Neill turned the helicopter toward them and a few minutes later it hovered above the mine itself.

Masses of squat mining equipment had made their way to the operations. Shafts had been sunk; empty carts waited in patient rows. A steady stream of loaded carts hurried toward the horizon, dribbling ore after them. Activity and the noise of machines hung over the area, an abrupt center of industry in the bleak wastes of slag.

"Here comes that exploring crew," Morrison observed, peering back the way they had come. "You think maybe they'll tangle?" He grinned. "No, I guess it's too much to hope for."

"It is this time," O'Neill answered. "They're looking for different substances, probably. And they're normally conditioned to ignore each other."

The first of the exploring bugs reached the line of ore carts. It veered slightly and continued its search; the carts traveled in their inexorable line as if nothing had happened.

Disappointed, Morrison turned away from the window and swore. "No use. It's like each doesn't exist for the other."

Gradually the exploring crew moved away from the line of carts, past the mining operations and over a ridge beyond. There was no special hurry; they departed without having reacted to the ore-gathering syndrome.

"Maybe they're from the same factory," Morrison said hopefully.

O'Neill pointed to the antennas visible on the major mining equipment. "Their vanes are turned at a different vector, so these represent two factories. It's going to be hard; we'll have to get it exactly right or there won't be any reaction." He clicked on the radio and got hold of the monitor at the settlement. "Any results on the consolidated back-order sheets?"

The operator put him through to the settlement governing offices.

"They're starting to come in," Perine told him. "As soon as we get sufficient samplings, we'll try to determine which raw materials which factories lack. It's going to be risky, trying to extrapolate from complex products. There may be a number of basic elements common to the various sublots."

"What happens when we've identified the missing element?" Morrison asked O'Neill. "What happens when we've got two tangent factories short on the same material?"

"Then," O'Neill said grimly, "we start collecting the material ourselves—even if we have to melt down every object in the settlements."

III

In the moth-ridden darkness of night, a dim wind stirred, chill and faint. Dense underbrush rattled metallically. Here and there a nocturnal rodent prowled, its senses hyperalert, peering, planning, seeking food.

The area was wild. No human settlements existed for miles; the entire region had been seared flat, cauterized by repeated H-bomb blasts. Somewhere in the murky darkness, a sluggish trickle of water made its way among slag and weeds, dripping thickly into what had once been an elaborate labyrinth of sewer mains. The pipes lay cracked and broken, jutting up into the night darkness, overgrown with creeping vegetation. The wind raised clouds of black ash that swirled and danced among the weeds. Once, an enormous mutant wren stirred sleepily, pulled its crude protective night coat of rags around it and again dozed off.

For a time, there was no movement. A streak of stars showed in the sky overhead, glowing starkly, remotely. Earl Perine shivered, peered up and huddled closer to the pulsing heat-element placed on the ground between the three men.

"Well?" Morrison challenged, teeth chattering.

O'Neill didn't answer. He finished his cigarette, crushed

it against a mound of decaying slag and, getting out his lighter, lit another. The mass of tungsten—the bait—lay a hundred yards directly ahead of them.

During the last few days, both the Detroit and Pittsburgh factories had run short of tungsten. And in at least one sector, their apparatus overlapped. This sluggish heap represented precision cutting tools, parts ripped from electrical switches, high-quality surgical equipment, sections of permanent magnets, measuring devices ... tungsten from every possible source, gathered feverishly from all the settlements.

Dark mist lay spread over the tungsten mound. Occasionally, a night moth fluttered down, attracted by the glow of reflected starlight. The moth hung momentarily, beat its elongated wings futilely against the interwoven tangle of metal and then drifted off, into the shadows of the thick-packed vines that rose up from the stumps of sewer pipes.

"Not a very damn pretty spot," Perine said wryly.

"Don't kid yourself," O'Neill retorted. "This is the prettiest spot on Earth. This is the spot that marks the grave of the autofac network. People are going to come around here looking for it someday. There's going to be a plaque here a mile high."

"You're trying to keep your morale up," Morrison snorted. "You don't believe they're going to slaughter themselves over a heap of surgical tools and light-bulb filaments. They've probably got a machine down in the bottom level that sucks tungsten out of rock."

"Maybe," O'Neill said, slapping at a mosquito. The insect dodged cannily and then buzzed over to annoy Perine. Perine swung viciously at it and squatted sullenly down against the damp vegetation.

And there was what they had come to see.

O'Neill realized with a start that he had been looking at

it for several minutes without recognizing it. The search-bug lay absolutely still. It rested at the crest of a small rise of slag, its anterior end slightly raised, receptors fully extended. It might have been an abandoned hulk; there was no activity of any kind, no sign of life or consciousness. The search-bug fitted perfectly into the wasted, fire-drenched landscape. A vague tub of metal sheets and gears and flat treads, it rested and waited. And watched.

It was examining the heap of tungsten. The bait had drawn its first bite.

"Fish," Perine said thickly. "The line moved. I think the sinker dropped."

"What the hell are you mumbling about?" Morrison grunted. Ane then he, too, saw the search-bug. "Jesus," he whispered. He half rose to his feet, massive body arched forward. "Well, there's *one* of them. Now all we need is a unit from the other factory. Which do you suppose it is?"

O'Neill located the communication vane and traced its angle. "Pittsburgh, so pray for Detroit . . . pray like mad."

Satisfied, the search-bug detached itself and rolled forward. Cautiously approaching the mound, it began a series of intricate maneuvers, rolling first one way and then another. The three watching men were mystified—until they glimpsed the first probing stalks of other search-bugs.

"Communication," O'Neill said softly. "Like bees."

Now five Pittsburgh search-bugs were approaching the mound of tungsten products. Receptors waving excitedly, they increased their pace, scurrying in a sudden burst of discovery up the side of the mound to the top. A bug burrowed and rapidly disappeared. The whole mound shuddered; the bug was down inside, exploring the extent of the find.

Ten minutes later, the first Pittsburgh ore carts appeared and began industriously hurrying off with their haul.

"Damn it!" O'Neill said, agonized. "They'll have it all before Detroit shows up."

"Can't we do anything to slow them down?" Perine demanded helplessly. Leaping to his feet, he grabbed up a rock and heaved it at the nearest cart. The rock bounced off and the cart continued its work, unperturbed.

O'Neill got to his feet and prowled around, body rigid with impotent fury. Where were they? The autofacs were equal in all respects and the spot was the exact same linear distance from each center. Theoretically, the parties should have arrived simultaneously. Yet there was no sign of Detroit—and the final pieces of tungsten were being loaded before his eyes.

But then something streaked past him.

He didn't recognize it, for the object moved too quickly. It shot like a bullet among the tangled vines, raced up the side of the hill-crest, poised for an instant to aim itself and hurtled down the far side. It smashed directly into the lead cart. Projectile and victim shattered in an abrupt burst of sound.

Morrison leaped up. "What the hell?"

"That's it!" Perine screamed, dancing around and waving his skinny arms. "It's Detroit!"

A second Detroit search-bug appeared, hesitated as it took in the situation, and then flung itself furiously at the retreating Pittsburgh carts. Fragments of tungsten scattered everywhere—parts, wiring, broken plates, gears and springs and bolts of the two antagonists flew in all directions. The remaining carts wheeled screechingly; one of them dumped its load and rattled off at top speed. A second followed, still weighed down with tungsten. A Detroit search-bug caught up with it, spun directly in its path and neatly overturned it. Bug and cart rolled down a shallow trench, into a stagnant pool of water. Dripping and glistening, the two of them struggled, half-submerged.

"Well," O'Neill said unsteadily, "we did it. We can start back home." His legs felt weak. "Where's our vehicle?"

As he gunned the truck motor, something flashed a long way off, something large and metallic, moving over the dead slag and ash. It was a dense clot of carts, a solid expanse of heavy-duty ore carriers racing to the scene. Which factory were they from?

It didn't matter, for out of the thick tangle of black dripping vines, a web of counterextensions was creeping to meet them. Both factories were assembling their mobile units. From all directions, bugs slithered and crept, closing in around the remaining heap of tungsten. Neither factory was going to let needed raw material get away; neither was going to give up its find. Blindly, mechanically, in the grip of inflexible directives, the two opponents labored to assemble superior forces.

"Come on," Morrison said urgently. "Let's get out of here. All hell is bursting loose."

O'Neill hastily turned the truck in the direction of the settlement. They began rumbling through the darkness on their way back. Every now and then, a metallic shape shot by them, going in the opposite direction.

"Did you see the load in that last cart?" Perine asked, worried. "It wasn't empty."

Neither were the carts that followed it, a whole procession of bulging supply carriers directed by an elaborate high-level surveying unit.

"Guns," Morrison said, eyes wide with apprehension. "They're taking in weapons. But who's going to use them?"

"They are," O'Neill answered. He indicated a movement to their right. "Look over there. This is something we hadn't expected."

They were seeing the first factory representative move into action.

As the truck pulled into the Kansas City settlement, Judith hurried breathlessly toward them. Fluttering in her hand was a strip of metal-foil paper.

"What is it?" O'Neill demanded, grabbing it from her.

"Just came." His wife struggled to catch her breath. "A mobile car—raced up, dropped it off—and left. Big excitement. Golly, the factory's—a blaze of lights. You can see it for miles."

O'Neill scanned the paper. It was a factory certification for the last group of settlement-placed orders, a total tabulation of requested and factory-analyzed needs. Stamped across the list in heavy black type were six foreboding words:

ALL SHIPMENTS SUSPENDED
UNTIL FURTHER NOTICE

Letting out his breath harshly, O'Neill handed the paper over to Perine. "No more consumer goods," he said ironically, a nervous grin twitching across his face. "The network's going on a wartime footing."

"Then we did it?" Morrison asked haltingly.

"That's right," O'Neill said. Now that the conflict had been sparked, he felt a growing, frigid terror. "Pittsburgh and Detroit are in it to the finish. It's too late for us to change our minds, now—they're lining up allies."

IV

Cool morning sunlight lay across the ruined plain of black metallic ash. The ash smoldered a dull, unhealthy red; it was still warm.

"Watch your step," O'Neill cautioned. Grabbing hold of his wife's arm, he led her from the rusty, sagging truck, up onto the top of a pile of strewn concrete blocks, the scattered remains of a pillbox installation. Earl Perine followed, making his way carefully, hesitantly.

Behind them, the dilapidated settlement lay spread out, a disorderly checkerboard of houses, buildings and streets. Since the autofac network had closed down its supply and maintenance, the human settlements had fallen into semi-barbarism. The commodities that remained were broken and only partly usable. It had been over a year since the last mobile factory truck had appeared, loaded with food, tools, clothing and repair parts. From the flat expanse of dark concrete and metal at the foot of the mountains, nothing had emerged in their direction.

Their wish had been granted—they were cut off, detached from the network.

On their own.

Around the settlement grew ragged fields of wheat and tattered stalks of sun-baked vegetables. Crude handmade tools had been distributed, primitive artifacts hammered out with great labor by the various settlements. The settlements were linked only by horse-drawn cart and by the slow stutter of the telegraph key.

They had managed to keep their organization, though. Goods and services were exchanged on a slow, steady basis. Basic commodities were produced and distributed. The clothing that O'Neill and his wife and Earl Perine wore was coarse and unbleached, but sturdy. And they had managed to convert a few of the trucks from gasoline to wood.

"Here we are," O'Neill said. "We can see from here."

"Is it worth it?" Judith asked, exhausted. Bending down, she plucked aimlessly at her shoe, trying to dig a pebble from the soft hide sole. "It's a long way to come, to see something we've seen every day for thirteen months."

"True," O'Neill admitted, his hand briefly resting on his wife's slim shoulder. "But this may be the last. And that's what we want to see."

In the gray sky above them, a swift circling dot of opaque black moved. High, remote, the dot spun and darted, following an intricate and wary course. Gradually, its gyrations moved it toward the mountains and the bleak expanse of bomb-rubbled structure sunk in their base.

"San Francisco," O'Neill explained. "One of those long-range hawk projectiles, all the way from the West Coast."

"And you think it's the last?" Perine asked.

"It's the only one we've seen this month." O'Neill seated himself and began sprinkling dried bits of tobacco into a trench of brown paper. "And we used to see hundreds."

"Maybe they have something better," Judith suggested. She found a smooth rock and tiredly seated herself. "Could it be?"

Her husband smiled ironically. "No. They don't have anything better."

The three of them were tensely silent. Above them, the circling dot of black drew closer. There was no sign of activity from the flat surface of metal and concrete; the Kansas City factory remained inert, totally unresponsive. A few billows of warm ash drifted across it and one end was partly submerged in rubble. The factory had taken numerous direct hits. Across the plain, the furrows of its subsurface tunnels lay exposed, clogged with debris and the dark, water-seeking tendrils of tough vines.

"Those damn vines," Perine grumbled, picking at an old sore on his unshaven chin. "They're taking over the world."

Here and there around the factory, the demolished ruin of a mobile extension rusted in the morning dew. Carts, trucks, search-bugs, factory representatives, weapons carriers, guns, supply trains, subsurface projectiles, indiscriminate parts of machinery mixed and fused together in shapeless piles. Some had been destroyed returning to the factory; others had been contacted as they emerged, fully loaded, heavy with equipment. The factory itself—what remained of it—seemed to have settled more deeply into the earth. Its upper surface was barely visible, almost lost in drifting ash.

In four days, there had been no known activity, no visible movement of any sort.

"It's dead," Perine said. "You can see it's dead."

O'Neill didn't answer. Squatting down, he made himself comfortable and prepared to wait. In his own mind, he was sure that some fragment of automation remained in the eroded factory. Time would tell. He examined his wristwatch; it was eight-thirty. In the old days, the factory would be starting its daily routine. Processions of trucks and varied mobile units would be coming to the surface, loaded with supplies, to begin their expeditions to the human settlement.

Off to the right, something stirred. He quickly turned his attention to it.

A single battered ore-gathering cart was creeping clumsily toward the factory. One last damaged mobile unit trying to complete its task. The cart was virtually empty; a few meager scraps of metal lay strewn in its hold. A scavenger ... the metal was sections ripped from destroyed equipment encountered on the way. Feebly, like a blind metallic insect, the cart approached the factory. Its progress was incredibly jerky. Every now and then, it halted, bucked and quivered, and wandered aimlessly off the path.

"Control is bad," Judith said, with a touch of horror in her voice. "The factory's having trouble guiding it back."

Yes, he had seen that. Around New York, the factory had lost its high-frequency transmitter completely. Its mobile units had floundered in crazy gyrations, racing in random circles, crashing against rocks and trees, sliding into gullies, overturning, finally unwinding and becoming reluctantly inanimate.

The ore cart reached the edge of the ruined plain and halted briefly. Above it, the dot of black still circled the sky. For a time, the cart remained frozen.

"The factory's trying to decide," Perine said. "It needs the material, but it's afraid of that hawk up there."

The factory debated and nothing stirred. Then the ore cart again resumed its unsteady crawl. It left the tangle of vines and started out across the blasted open plain. Painfully, with infinite caution, it headed toward the slab of dark concrete and metal at the base of the mountains.

The hawk stopped circling.

"Get down!" O'Neill said sharply. "They've got those rigged with the new bombs."

His wife and Perine crouched down beside him and the three of them peered warily at the plain and the metal insect crawling laboriously across it. In the sky, the hawk swept in a straight line until it hung directly over the cart. Then, without sound or warning, it came down in a straight dive.

Hands to her face, Judith shrieked, "I can't watch! It's *awful!* Like wild animals!"

"It's not after the cart," O'Neill grated.

As the airborne projectile dropped, the cart put on a burst of desperate speed. It raced noisily toward the factory, clanking and rattling, trying in a last futile attempt to reach safety. Forgetting the menace above, the frantically eager factory opened up and guided its mobile unit directly inside. And the hawk had what it wanted.

Before the barrier could close, the hawk swooped down in a long glide parallel with the ground. As the cart disappeared into the depths of the factory, the hawk shot after it, a swift shimmer of metal that hurtled past the clanking cart. Suddenly aware, the factory snapped the barrier shut. Grotesquely, the cart struggled; it was caught fast in the half-closed entrance.

But whether it freed itself didn't matter. There was a dull, rumbling stir. The ground moved, billowed, then settled back. A deep shock wave passed beneath the three watching human beings. From the factory rose a single column of black smoke. The surface of concrete split; like a dried pod, it shriveled and broke, and dribbled shattered bits of itself in a shower of ruin. The smoke hung for a while, drifting aimlessly away with the morning wind.

The factory was a fused, gutted wreck. It had been penetrated and destroyed.

O'Neill got stiffly to his feet. "That's that. All over with. We've got what we set out after—we've destroyed the autofac network." He glanced at Perine. "Or *was* that what we were after?"

They looked toward the settlement that lay behind them. Little remained of the orderly rows of houses and streets of the previous year. Without the network, the settlement had rapidly decayed. The original prosperous neatness had dissipated; the settlement was shabby, ill-kept.

"Of course," Perine said haltingly. "Once we get into the factories and start setting up our own assembly lines. . . ."

"Is there anything left?" Judith inquired.

"There must be something left. My God, there were levels going down *miles!*"

"Some of those bombs they developed toward the end were awfully big," Judith pointed out. "Better than anything we had in our war."

"Remember that camp we saw? The ruins-squatters?"

"I wasn't along," Perine said.

"They were like wild animals. Eating roots and larvae. Sharpening rocks, tanning hides. Savagery. Bestiality."

"But that's what people like that want," Perine answered defensively.

"Do they? Do we want this?" O'Neill indicated the straggling settlement. "Is this what we set out looking for, that day we collected the tungsten? Or that day we told the factory truck its milk was—" He couldn't remember the word.

"Pizzled," Judith supplied.

"Come on," O'Neill said. "Let's get started. Let's see what's left of that factory—left for us."

They approached the ruined factory late in the afternoon. Four trucks rumbled shakily up to the rim of the gutted pit and halted, motors steaming, tailpipes dripping. Wary and alert, workmen scrambled down and stepped gingerly across the hot ash.

"Maybe it's too soon," one of them objected.

O'Neill had no intention of waiting. "Come on," he ordered. Grabbing up a flashlight, he stepped down into the crater.

The shattered hull of the Kansas City factory lay directly ahead. In its gutted mouth, the ore cart still hung caught, but it was no longer struggling. Beyond the cart was an ominous pool of gloom. O'Neill flashed his light through the entrance; the tangled, jagged remains of upright supports were visible.

"We want to get down deep," he said to Morrison, who prowled cautiously beside him. "If there's anything left, it's at the bottom."

Morrison grunted. "Those boring moles from Atlanta got most of the deep layers."

"Until the others got their mines sunk." O'Neill stepped carefully through the sagging entrance, climbed a heap of debris that had been tossed against the slit from inside, and found himself within the factory—an expanse of confused wreckage, without pattern or meaning.

"Entropy," Morrison breathed, oppressed. "The thing it always hated. The thing it was built to fight. Random particles everywhere. No purpose to it."

"Down underneath," O'Neill said stubbornly, "we may find some sealed enclaves. I know they got so they were dividing up into autonomous sections, trying to preserve repair units intact, to reform the composite factory."

"The moles got most of them, too," Morrison observed, but he lumbered after O'Neill.

Behind them, the workmen came slowly. A section of wreckage shifted ominously and a shower of hot fragments cascaded down.

"You men get back to the trucks," O'Neill said. "No sense endangering any more of us than we have to. If Morrison and I don't come back, forget us—don't risk sending a rescue party." As they left, he pointed out to Morrison a descending ramp still partially intact. "Let's get below."

Silently, the two men passed one dead level after another. Endless miles of dark ruin stretched out, without sound or activity. The vague shapes of darkened machinery, unmoving belts and conveyer equipment were partially visible, and the partially completed husks of war projectiles, bent and twisted by the final blast.

"We can salvage some of that," O'Neill said, but he didn't actually believe it. The machinery was fused, shapeless. Everything in the factory had run together, molten slag without form or use. "Once we get it to the surface ... "

"We can't," Morrison contradicted bitterly. "We don't have hoists or winches." He kicked at a heap of charred supplies that had stopped along its broken belt and spilled halfway across the ramp.

"It seemed like a good idea at the time," O'Neill said as

the two of them continued past the vacant levels of inert machines. "But now that I look back, I'm not so sure."

They had penetrated a long way into the factory. The final level lap spread out ahead of them. O'Neill flashed the light here and there, trying to locate undestroyed sections, portions of the assembly process still intact.

It was Morrison who felt it first. He suddenly dropped to his hands and knees; heavy body pressed against the floor, he lay listening, face hard, eyes wide. "For God's sake—"

"What is it?" O'Neill cried. Then he, too, felt it. Beneath them, a faint, insistent vibration hummed through the floor, a steady hum of activity. They had been wrong; the hawk had not been totally successful. Below, in a deeper level, the factory was still alive. Closed, limited operations still went on.

"On its own," O'Neill muttered, searching for an extension of the descent lift. "Autonomous activity, set to continue after the rest is gone. How do we get down?"

The descent lift was broken off, sealed by a thick section of metal. The still-living layer beneath their feet was completely cut off; there was no entrance.

Racing back the way they had come, O'Neill reached the surface and hailed the first truck. "Where the hell's the torch? Give it here!"

The precious blowtorch was passed to him and he hurried back, puffing, into the depths of the ruined factory, where Morrison waited. Together, the two of them began frantically cutting through the warped metal flooring, burning apart the sealed layers of protective mesh.

"It's coming," Morrison gasped, squinting in the glare of the torch. The plate fell with a clang, disappearing into the level below. A blaze of white light burst up around them and the two men leaped back.

In the sealed chamber, furious activity boomed and

echoed, a steady process of moving belts, whirring ma-
chine-tools, fast-moving mechanical supervisors. At one
end, a steady flow of raw materials entered the line; at the
far end, the final product was whipped off, inspected and
crammed into a conveyer tube.

All this was visible for a split second; then the intrusion
was discovered. Robot relays closed as automatic reflexes
came into play. The blaze of lights flickered and dimmed.
The assembly line froze to a halt, stopped in its furious
activity.

The machines clicked off and became silent.

At one end, a mobile unit detached itself and sped up
the wall toward the hole O'Neill and Morrison had cut. It
slammed an emergency seal in place and expertly welded
it tight. The scene below was gone. A moment later the
floor shivered as activity resumed.

Morrison, white-faced and shaking, turned to O'Neill.
"What are they doing? What are they making?"

"Not weapons," O'Neill said.

"That stuff is being sent up"—Morrison gestured con-
vulsively—"to the surface."

Shakily, O'Neill climbed to his feet. "Can we locate the
spot?"

"I—think so."

"We better." O'Neill swept up the flashlight and started
toward the ascent ramp. "We're going to have to see what
those pellets are that they're shooting up."

The exit valve of the conveyer tube was concealed in a
tangle of vines and ruins a quarter of a mile beyond the
factory. In a slot of rock at the base of the mountains, the
valve poked up like a nozzle. From ten yards away, it was
invisible; the two men were almost on top of it before they
noticed it.

Every few moments, a pellet burst from the valve and
shot up into the sky. The nozzle revolved and altered its

angle of deflection; each pellet was launched in a slightly varied trajectory.

"How far are they going?" Morrison wondered.

"Probably varies. It's distributing them at random." O'Neill advanced cautiously, but the mechanism took no notice of him. Plastered against the towering wall of rock was a crumpled pellet; by accident, the nozzle had released it directly at the mountainside. O'Neill climbed up, got it and jumped down.

The pellet was a smashed container of machinery, tiny metallic elements too minute to be analyzed without a microscope.

"Not a weapon," O'Neill said. The cylinder had split. At first he couldn't tell if it had been the impact or deliberate internal mechanisms at work. From the rent, an ooze of metal bits was sliding. Squatting down, O'Neill examined them.

The bits were in motion. Microscopic machinery, smaller than ants, smaller than pins, working energetically, purposefully—constructing something that looked like a tiny rectangle of steel.

"They're building," O'Neill said, awed. He got up and prowled on. Off to the side, at the far edge of the gully, he came across a downed pellet far advanced on its construction. Apparently it had been released some time ago.

This one had made great enough progress to be identified. Minute as it was, the structure was familiar. The machinery was building a miniature replica of the demolished factory.

"Well," O'Neill said thoughtfully, "we're back where we started from. For better or worse . . . I don't know."

"I guess they must be all over Earth by now," Morrison said, "landing everywhere and going to work."

A thought struck O'Neill. "Maybe some of them are geared to escape velocity. That would be neat—autofac networks throughout the whole universe."

Behind him, the nozzle continued to spurt out its torrent of metal seeds.

Adam and No Eve

ALFRED BESTER

This story by the celebrated author of The Demolished Man *and* The Stars My Destination *was first published more than thirty years ago, and we know now that its central situation—a secret rocket flight by a private inventor—is unlikely to occur. Going into space is an expensive proposition, feasible only for nations and perhaps some giant corporations, and free-lance experiments of this kind are out of the question. Aside from that, though, the story remains valid and powerful—for it reminds us once again of the ecological fragility of our planet's environment, and in dramatic, powerful style sounds an alarm against those who rush heedlessly forward, blindly waving the banners of progress.*

CRANE KNEW this must be the seacoast. Instinct told him; but more than instinct, the few shreds of knowledge that clung to his torn, feverish brain told him; the stars that had shown at night through the rare breaks in the clouds, and his compass that still pointed a trembling finger north. That was strangest of all, Crane thought. Though a welter of chaos, the Earth still retained its polarity.

It was no longer a coast; there was no longer any sea. Only the faint line of what had been a cliff, stretching north and south for endless miles. A line of gray ash. The same gray ash and cinders that lay behind him; the same gray ash that stretched before him. Fine silt, knee-deep, that swirled up at every motion and choked him. Cinders that scudded in dense mighty clouds when the mad winds blew. Cinders that were churned to viscous mud when the frequent rains fell.

The sky was jet overhead. The black clouds rode high and were pierced with shafts of sunlight that marched swiftly over the Earth. Where the light struck a cinder storm, it was filled with gusts of dancing, gleaming particles. Where it played through rain it brought the arches of rainbows into being. Rain fell; cinder-storms blew; light thrust down—together, alternately and continually in a jigsaw of black and white violence. So it had been for months. So it was over every mile of the broad Earth.

Crane passed the edge of the ashen cliffs and began crawling down the even slope that had once been the ocean bed. He had been traveling so long that all sense of pain had left him. He braced elbows and dragged his body forward. Then he brought his right knee under him and reached forward with elbows again. Elbows, knee, elbows, knee— He had forgotten what it was to walk.

Life, he thought dazedly, is wonderful. It adapts itself to anything. If it must crawl, it crawls. Callus forms on the elbows and knees. The neck and shoulders toughen. The nostrils learn to snort away the ashes before they inhale. The bad leg swells and festers. It numbs, and presently it will rot and fall off.

"I beg pardon," Crane said, "I didn't quite get that—"

He peered up at the tall figure before him and tried to understand the words. It was Hallmyer. He wore his stained lab jacket and his gray hair was awry. Hallmyer stood delicately on top of the ashes and Crane wondered why he could see the scudding cinder clouds through his body.

"How do you like your world, Stephen?" Hallmyer asked.

Crane shook his head miserably.

"Not very pretty, eh?" said Hallmyer. "Look around you. Dust, that's all; dust and ashes. Crawl, Stephen, crawl. You'll find nothing but dust and ashes—"

Hallmyer produced a goblet of water from nowhere. It was clear and cold. Crane could see the fine mist of dew on its surface and his mouth was suddenly coated with dry grit.

"Hallmyer!" he cried. He tried to get to his feet and reach for the water, but the jolt of pain in his right leg warned him. He crouched back.

Hallmyer sipped and then spat in his face. The water felt warm.

"Keep crawling," said Hallmyer bitterly. "Crawl round and round the face of the Earth. You'll find nothing but dust and ashes—" He emptied the goblet on the ground before Crane. "Keep crawling. How many miles? Figure it out for yourself. Pi-R-Square. The radius is eight thousand or so—"

He was gone, jacket and goblet. Crane realized that rain was falling again. He pressed his face into the warm sodden cinder mud, opened his mouth and tried to suck the moisture. He groaned and presently began crawling.

There was an instinct that drove him on. He had to get somewhere. It was associated, he knew, with the sea—with the edge of the sea. At the shore of the sea something waited for him. Something that would help him understand all this. He had to get to the sea—that is, if there was a sea any more.

The thundering rain beat his back like heavy planks. Crane paused and yanked the knapsack around to his side where he probed in it with one hand. It contained exactly three things. A pistol, a bar of chocolate and a can of peaches. All that was left of two months' supplies. The chocolate was pulpy and spoiled. Crane knew he had best eat it before all value rotted away. But in another day he would lack the strength to open the can. He pulled it out and attacked it with the opener. By the time he had pierced and pried away a flap of tin, the rain had passed.

As he munched the fruit and sipped the juice, he watched the wall of rain marching before him down the slope of the ocean bed. Torrents of water were gushing through the mud. Small channels had already been cut—channels that would be new rivers some day. A day he would never see. A day that no living thing would ever see. As he flipped the empty can aside, Crane thought: The last living thing on Earth eats its last meal. Metabolism plays its last act.

Wind would follow the rain. In the endless weeks that he had been crawling, he had learned that. Wind would come in a few minutes and flog him with its clouds of cinders and ashes. He crawled forward, bleary eyes searching the flat gray miles for cover.

Evelyn tapped his shoulder.

Crane knew it was she before he turned his head. She stood alongside, fresh and gay in her bright dress, but her lovely face was puckered with alarm.

"Stephen," she cried, "you've got to hurry!"

He could only admire the way her smooth honey hair waved to her shoulders.

"Oh, darling!" she said, "you've been hurt!" Her quick gentle hands touched his legs and back. Crane nodded.

"Got it landing," he said. "I wasn't used to a parachute. I always thought you came down gently—like plumping onto a bed. But the gray earth came up at me like a fist— And Umber was fighting around in my arms. I couldn't let him drop, could I?"

"Of course not, dear—" Evelyn said.

"So I just held on to him and tried to get my legs under me," Crane said. "And then something smashed my legs and side—"

He paused, wondering how much she knew of what really had happened. He didn't want to frighten her.

"Evelyn, darling—" he said, trying to reach up his arms.

"No dear," she said. She looked back in fright. "You've got to hurry. You've got to watch out behind!"

"The cinder storms?" He grimaced. "I've been through them before."

"Not the storms!" Evelyn cried. "Something else. Oh, Stephen—"

Then she was gone, but Crane knew she had spoken the truth. There was something behind—something that had been following him all those weeks. Far in the back of his mind he had sensed the menace. It was closing in on him like a shroud. He shook his head. Somehow that was impossible. He was the last living thing on Earth. How could there be a menace?

The wind roared behind him, and an instant later came the heavy clouds of cinders and ashes. They lashed over him, biting his skin. With dimming eyes, he saw the way they coated the mud and covered it with a fine dry carpet. Crane drew his knees under him and covered his head with his arms. With the knapsack as a pillow, he prepared to wait out the storm. It would pass as quickly as the rain.

The storm whipped up a great bewilderment in his sick head. Like a child he pushed at the pieces of his memory, trying to fit them together. Why was Hallmyer so bitter toward him? It couldn't have been that argument, could it?

What argument?

Why, that one before all this happened.

Oh, that!

Abruptly, the pieces fitted themselves together.

Crane stood alongside the sleek lines of his ship and admired it tremendously. The roof of the shed had been removed and the nose of the ship hoisted so that it rested on a cradle pointed toward the sky. A workman was carefully burnishing the inner surfaces of the rocket jets.

The muffled sounds of an argument came from within the ship and then a heavy clanking. Crane ran up the short iron ladder to the port and thrust his head inside. A few feet beneath him, two men were buckling the long tanks of ferrous solution into place.

"Easy there," Crane called. "Want to knock the ship apart?" One looked up and grinned. Crane knew what he was thinking. That the ship would tear itself apart. Everyone said that. Everyone except Evelyn. She had faith in him. Hallmyer never said it either. But Hallmyer thought he was crazy in another way. As he descended the ladder, Crane saw Hallmyer come into the shed, lab jacket flying.

"Speak of the devil!" Crane muttered.

Hallmyer began shouting as soon as he saw Crane. "Now listen—"

"Not all over again," Crane said.

Hallmyer dug a sheaf of papers out of his pocket and waved it under Crane's nose.

"I've been up half the night," he said, "working it through again. I tell you I'm right. I'm absolutely right—"

Crane looked at the tight-written equations and then at Hallmyer's bloodshot eyes. The man was half mad with fear.

"For the last time," Hallmyer went on. "You're using your new catalyst on iron solution. All right. I grant that it's a miraculous discovery. I give you credit for that."

Miraculous was hardly the word for it. Crane knew that without conceit, for he realized he'd only stumbled on it. You had to stumble on a catalyst that would induce atomic disintegration of iron and give 10×10^{10} foot-pounds of energy for every gram of fuel. No man was smart enough to think all that up by himself.

"You don't think I'll make it?" Crane asked.

"To the Moon? Around the Moon? Maybe. You've got a fifty-fifty chance." Hallmyer ran fingers through his lank hair. "But for God's sake, Stephen, I'm not worried about you. If you want to kill yourself, that's your own affair. It's the Earth I'm worried about—"

"Nonsense. Go home and sleep it off."

"Look"—Hallmyer pointed to the sheets of paper with a shaky hand—"no matter how you work the feed and mixing system you can't get one hundred percent efficiency in the mixing and discharge."

"That's what makes it a fifty-fifty chance," Crane said. "So what's bothering you?"

"The catalyst that will escape through the rocket tubes. Do you realize what it'll do if a drop hits the Earth? It'll start a chain of iron disintegrations that'll envelope the globe. It'll reach out to every iron atom—and there's iron everywhere. There won't be any Earth left for you to return to—"

"Listen," Crane said wearily, "we've been through all this before." He took Hallmyer to the base of the rocket cradle. Beneath the iron framework was a two-hundred-foot pit, fifty feet wide and lined with firebrick.

"That's for the initial discharge flames. If any of the catalyst goes through, it'll be trapped in this pit and taken care of by the secondary reactions. Satisfied now?"

"But while you're in flight," Hallmyer persisted, "you'll be endangering the Earth until you're beyond Roche's limit. Every drop of non-activated catalyst will eventually sink back to the ground and—"

"For the very last time," Crane said grimly, "the flame of the rocket discharge takes care of that. It will envelop any escaped particles and destroy them. Now get out. I've got work to do."

As he pushed him to the door, Hallmyer screamed and waved his arms. "I won't let you do it!" he repeated over and over. "I'll find some way to stop you, I won't let you do it—"

Work? No, it was sheer intoxication to labor over the

ship. It had the fine beauty of a well-made thing. The
beauty of polished armor, of a balanced swept-hilt rapier,
of a pair of matched guns. There was no thought of
danger and death in Crane's mind as he wiped his hands
with rags after the last touches were finished.

She lay in the cradle ready to pierce the skies. Fifty feet
of slender steel, the rivet heads gleaming like jewels.
Thirty feet were given over to fuel the catalyst. Most of
the forward compartment contained the spring hammock
Crane had devised to take up the initial acceleration
shock. The ship's nose was a solid mass of natural quartz
that stared upward like a cyclopian eye.

Crane thought: She'll die after this trip. She'll return to
the Earth and smash in a blaze of fire and thunder, for
there's no way yet of devising a safe landing for a rocket
ship. But it's worth it. She'll have had her one great flight,
and that's all any of us should want. One great beautiful
flight into the unknown—

As he locked the workshop door, Crane heard Hallmyer shouting from the cottage across the fields. Through
the evening gloom he could see him waving frantically.
He trotted through the crisp stubble, breathing the sharp
air deeply, grateful to be alive.

"It's Evelyn on the phone," Hallmyer said.

Crane stared at him. Hallmyer was acting peculiarly.
He refused to meet his eyes.

"What's the idea?" Crane asked. "I thought we agreed
that she wasn't to call—wasn't to get in touch with me
until I was ready to start? You been putting ideas into her
head? Is this the way you're going to stop me?"

Hallmyer said: "No—" and studiously examined the
indigo horizon.

Crane went into his study and picked up the phone.

"Now listen, darling," he said without preamble,
"there's no sense getting alarmed now. I explained everything very carefully. Just before the ship crashes, I take to

a parachute and float down as happy and gentle as Wynken, Blynken and Nod. I love you very much and I'll see you Wednesday when I start. So long—"

"Good-by, sweetheart," Evelyn's clear voice said, "and is that what you called me for?"

"Called you!"

A brown hulk disengaged itself from the hearth rug and lifted itself to strong legs. Umber, Crane's Great Dane, sniffed and cocked an ear. Then he whined.

"Did you say I called you?" Crane shouted.

Umber's throat suddenly poured forth a bellow. He reached Crane in a single bound, looked up into his face and whined and roared all at once.

"Shut up, you monster!" Crane said. He pushed Umber away with his foot.

"Give Umber a kick for me," Evelyn laughed. "Yes, dear. Someone called and said you wanted to speak to me."

"They did, eh? Look, honey, I'll call you back—"

Crane hung up. He arose doubtfully and watched Umber's uneasy actions. Through the windows, the late evening glow sent flickering shadows of orange light. Umber gazed at the light, sniffed and bellowed again. Suddenly struck, Crane leaped to the window.

Across the fields a solid mass of flame thrust high into the air, and within it was the fast-crumbling walls of the workshop. Silhouetted against the blaze, the figures of half a dozen men darted and ran.

"Good heavens!" Crane cried.

He shot out of the cottage and with Umber hard at his heels, sprinted toward the shed. As he ran he could see the graceful nose of the spaceship within the core of heat, still looking cool and untouched. If only he could reach it before the flames softened its metal and started the rivets.

The workmen trotted up to him, grimy and panting.

Crane gaped at them in a mixture of fury and bewilderment.

"Hallmyer!" he shouted. "Hallmyer!"

Hallmyer pushed through the crowd. His eyes were wild and gleamed with triumph.

"Too bad," he said. "I'm sorry. Stephen—"

"You swine!" Crane shouted. "You frightened old man!" He grasped Hallmyer by the lapels and shook him just once. Then he dropped him and started into the shed.

Hallmyer cried something and an instant later a body hurtled against Crane's calves and spilled him to the ground. He lurched to his feet, fists swinging. Umber was alongside, growling over the roar of the flames. Crane smashed a man in the face, and saw him stagger back against a second. He lifted a knee in a vicious drive that sent the last man crumpling to the ground. Then he ducked his head and plunged into the shop.

The scorch felt cool at first, but when he reached the ladder and began mounting to the port, he screamed with the agony of his burns. Umber was howling at the foot of the ladder, and Crane realized that the dog could never escape from the rocket blasts. He reached down and hauled Umber into the ship.

Crane was reeling as he closed and locked the port. He retained consciousness barely long enough to settle himself in the spring hammock. Then instinct alone prompted his hands to reach out toward the control board. Instinct and the frenzied refusal to let his beautiful ship waste itself in the flames. He would fail— Yes. But he would fail, trying.

His fingers tripped the switches. The ship shuddered and roared. And blackness descended over him.

How long was he unconscious? There was no telling. Crane awoke with cold pressing against his face and body, and the sound of frightened yelps in his ears. Crane looked up and saw Umber tangled in the springs and straps of the hammock. His first impulse was to laugh; then suddenly he realized. He had looked *up!* He had looked up at the hammock.

He was lying curled in the cup of the quartz nose. The ship had risen high—perhaps almost to Roche's zone, to the limit of the Earth's gravitational attraction, but then without guiding hands at the controls to continue its flight, had turned and was dropping back toward Earth. Crane peered through the crystal and gasped.

Below him was the ball of the Earth. It looked three times the size of the Moon. And it was no longer his Earth. It was a globe of fire mottled with black clouds. At the northernmost pole there was a tiny patch of white, and even as Crane watched, it was suddenly blotted over with hazy tones of red, scarlet and crimson. Hallmyer had been right.

He lay frozen in the cup of the nose for hours as the ship descended, watching the flames gradually fade away to leave nothing but the dense blanket of black around the Earth. He lay numb with horror, unable to understand— unable to reckon up a billion people snuffed out, a green fair planet reduced to ashes and cinders. His family, home, friends, everything that was once dear and close to him—gone. He could not think of Evelyn.

Air, whistling outside, awoke some instinct in him. The few shreds of reason left told him to go down with his ship and forget everything in the thunder and destruction, but the instinct of life forced him to his feet. He climbed up to the store chest and prepared for the landing. Parachute, a small oxygen tank—a knapsack of supplies. Only half aware of what he was doing he dressed for the descent, buckled on the 'chute and opened the port. Umber whined pathetically, and he took the heavy dog in his arms and stepped out into space.

But space hadn't been so clogged, the way it was now.

Then it had been difficult to breath. But that was because
the air had been rare—not filled with dry clogging grit like
now.

Every breath was a lungful of ground glass—or ashes—
or cinders—

The pieces of memory sagged apart. Abruptly he was in
the present again—a dense black present that hugged him
with soft weight and made him fight for breath. Crane
struggled in mad panic, and then relaxed.

It had happened before. A long time past he'd been
buried deep under ashes when he'd stopped to remember.
Weeks ago—or days—or months. Crane clawed with his
hands, inching forward through the mound of cinders that
the wind had thrown over him. Presently he emerged into
the light again. The wind had died away. It was time to
begin his crawl to the sea once more.

The vivid pictures of his memory scattered again before
the grim vista that stretched out ahead. Crane scowled. He
remembered too much, and too often. He had the vague
hope that if he remembered hard enough, he might change
one of the things he had done—just a very little thing—
and then all this would become untrue. He thought: It
might help if everyone remembered and wished at the
same time—but there isn't any more everyone. I'm the
only one. I'm the last memory on Earth. I'm the last life.

He crawled. Elbows, knee, elbows, knee— And then
Hallmyer was crawling alongside and making a great
game of it. He chortled and plunged in the cinders like a
happy sea lion.

Crane said: "But why do we have to get to the sea?"

Hallmyer blew a spume of ashes.

"Ask her," he said, pointing to Crane's other side.

Evelyn was there, crawling seriously, intently; mimick-
ing Crane's smallest action.

"It's because of our house," she said. "You remember
our house, darling? High on the cliff. We were going to

live there forever and ever, breathing the ozone and taking morning dips. I was there when you left. Now you're coming back to the house at the edge of the sea. Your beautiful flight is over, dear, and you're coming back to me. We'll live together, just we two, like Adam and Eve—"

Crane said: "That's nice."

Then Evelyn turned her head and screamed: "Oh, Stephen! Watch out!" and Crane felt the menace closing in on him again. Still crawling, he stared back at the vast gray plains of ash, and saw nothing. When he looked at Evelyn again he saw only his shadow, sharp and black. Presently, it, too, faded away as the marching shaft of sunlight passed.

But the dread remained. Evelyn had warned him twice, and she was always right. Crane stopped and turned, and settled himself to watch. If he was really being followed, he would see whatever it was, coming along his tracks.

There was a painful moment of lucidity. It cleaved through his fever and bewilderment, bringing with it the sharpness and strength of a knife.

I'm going mad, he thought. The corruption in my leg has spread to my brain. There is no Evelyn, no Hallmyer, no menace. In all this land there is no life but mine—and even ghosts and spirits of the underworld must have perished in the inferno that girdled the planet. No—there is nothing but me and my sickness. I'm dying—and when I perish, everything will perish. Only a mass of lifeless cinders will go on.

But there was a movement.

Instinct again. Crane dropped his head and played dead. Through slitted eyes he watched the ashen plains, wondering if death was playing tricks with his eyes. Another façade of rain was beating down toward him, and he

hoped he could make sure before all vision was obliter-
ated.

Yes. There.

A quarter mile back, a gray-brown shape was flitting
along the gray surface. Despite the drone of the distant
rain, Crane could hear the whisper of trodden cinders and
see the little clouds kicking up. Stealthily he groped for
the revolver in the knapsack as his mind reached feebly
for explanations and recoiled from fear.

The thing approached, and suddenly Crane squinted
and understood. He recalled Umber kicking with fear and
springing away from him when the 'chute landed them on
the ashen face of the Earth.

"Why, it's Umber," he murmured. He raised himself.
The dog halted. "Here, boy!" Crane croaked gaily. "Here,
boy!"

He was overcome with joy. He realized that a miserable
loneliness had hung over him, almost a horrible sensation
of oneness in emptiness. Now his was not the only life.
There was another. A friendly life that could offer love
and companionship. Hope kindled again.

"Here, boy!" he repeated. "Come on, boy—"

After a while he stopped trying to snap his fingers. The
Great Dane hung back, showing fangs and a lolling
tongue. The dog was emaciated to a skeleton and its eyes
gleamed red and ugly in the dusk. As Crane called once
more, mechanically, the dog snarled. Puffs of ash leaped
beneath its nostrils.

He's hungry, Crane thought, that's all. He reached into
the knapsack and at the gesture the dog snarled again.
Crane withdrew the chocolate bar and laboriously peeled
off the paper and silver foil. Weakly he tossed it toward
Umber. It fell far short. After a minute of savage uncertainty, the dog advanced slowly and gobbled up the food.
Ashes powdered its muzzle. It licked its chops ceaselessly
and continued to advance on Crane.

Panic jerked within him. A voice persisted: This is no friend. He has no love or companionship for you. Love and companionship have vanished from the land along with life. Now there is nothing left but hunger.

"No—" Crane whispered. "That isn't right. We're the last of life on Earth. It isn't right that we should tear at each other and seek to devour—"

But Umber was advancing with a slinking sidle, and his teeth showed sharp and white. And even as Crane stared at him, the dog snarled and lunged.

Crane thrust up an arm under the dog's muzzle, but the weight of the charge carried him backward. He cried out in agony as his broken, swollen leg was struck by the weight of the dog. With his free right hand he struck weakly, again and again, scarcely feeling the grind of teeth gnawing his left arm. Then something metallic was pressed under him and he realized he was lying on the revolver he had let fall.

He groped for it and prayed the cinders had not clogged its mechanism. As Umber let go his arm and tore at his throat, Crane brought the gun up and jabbed the muzzle blindly against the dog's body. He pulled and pulled the trigger until the roars died away and only empty clicks sounded. Umber shuddered in the ashes before him, his body nearly shot in two. Thick scarlet stained the gray.

Evelyn and Hallmyer looked down sadly at the broken animal. Evelyn was crying, and Hallmyer reached nervous fingers through his hair in the same old gesture.

"This is the finish, Stephen," he said. "You've killed part of yourself. Oh—you'll go on living, but not all of you. You'd best bury that corpse, Stephen. It's the corpse of your soul."

"I can't," Crane said. "The wind will blow the ashes away."

"Then burn it—"

It seemed that they helped him thrust the dead dog into his knapsack. They helped him take off his clothes and pack them underneath. They cupped their hands around the matches until the cloth caught fire, and blew on the weak flame until it sputtered and burned limply. Crane crouched by the fire and nursed it until nothing was left but more gray ash. Then he turned and once again began crawling down the ocean bed. He was naked now. There was nothing left of what had been but his flickering little life.

He was too heavy with sorrow to notice the furious rain that slammed and buffeted him, or the searing pains that were shooting through his blackened leg and up his hip. He crawled. Elbows, knee, elbows, knee— Woodenly, mechanically, apathetic to everything. To the latticed skies, the dreary ashen plains and even the dull glint of water that lay far ahead.

He knew it was the sea—what was left of the old, or a new one in the making. But it would be an empty, lifeless sea that some day would lap against a dry, lifeless shore. This would be a planet of rock and stone, of metal and snow and ice and water, but that would be all. No more life. He, alone, was useless. He was Adam, but there was no Eve.

Evelyn waved gaily to him from the shore. She was standing alongside the white cottage with the wind snapping her dress to show the clean, slender lines of her figure. And when he came a little closer, she ran out to him and helped him. She said nothing—only placed her hands under his shoulders and helped him lift the weight of his heavy pain-ridden body. And so at last he reached the sea.

It was real. He understood that. For even after Evelyn and the cottage had vanished, he felt the cool waters bathe his face. Quietly—Calmly—

Here's the sea, Crane thought, and here am I. Adam and no Eve. It's hopeless.

He rolled a little farther into the waters. They laved his torn body. Quietly—Calmly—

He lay with face to the sky, peering at the high menacing heavens, and the bitterness within him welled up.

"It's not right!" he cried. "It's not right that all this should pass away. Life is too beautiful to perish at the mad act of one mad creature—"

Quietly the waters laved him. Quietly—Calmly—

The sea rocked him gently, and even the agony that was reaching up toward his heart was no more than a gloved hand. Suddenly the skies split apart—for the first time in all those months—and Crane stared up at the stars.

Then he knew. This was not the end of life. There could never be an end to life. Within his body, within the rotting tissues that were rocking gently in the sea was the source of ten million-million lives. Cells—tissues—bacteria—endamoeba—Countless infinities of life that would take new root in the waters and live long after he was gone.

They would live on his rotting remains. They would feed on each other. They would adapt themselves to the new environment and feed on the minerals and sediments washed into this new sea. They would grow, burgeon, evolve. Life would reach out to the lands once more. It would begin again the same old re-repeated cycle that had begun perhaps with the rotting corpse of some last survivor of interstellar travel. It would happen over and over in the future ages.

And then he knew what had brought him back to the sea. There need be no Adam—no Eve. Only the sea, the great mother of life was needed. The sea had called him back to her depths that presently life might emerge once more, and he was content.

Quietly the waters rocked him. Quietly—Calmly—the mother of life rocked the last-born of the old cycle who would become the first-born of the new. And with glazing eyes Stephen Crane smiled up at the stars, stars that were sprinkled evenly across the sky. Stars that had not yet formed into the familiar constellations, nor would not for another hundred million centuries.

City of Yesterday

TERRY CARR

This is the story of a machine named Charles and a man named J-1001011. Both are deadly, the machine more so than the man. But this tightly told little tale depicts for us mankind's most sinister invention, more dangerous than any machine: blind patriotic discipline, mindless loyalty—a force that drives humanity to its most terrible crimes.

Terry Carr is a lanky Californian who, in a distinguished career as an editor, was responsible for publishing some of the most memorable science fiction books of the 1960's. Now, having given up editing in favor of writing, he's likely to make an equally valuable contribution to science fiction in the 1970's and beyond.

"WAKE up," said Charles, and J-1001011 instantly sat up. The couch sat up with him, jackknifing to form his pilot's seat. J-1001011 noted that the seat was in combat position, raised high enough to give him an unobstructed vision on all sides of the planetflier.

"We're in orbit around our objective," said Charles. "Breakout and attack in seven minutes. Eat. Eliminate."

J-1001011 obediently withdrew the red-winking tube from the panel before him and put it between his lips. Warm, mealy liquid fed into his mouth, and he swallowed at a regular rate. When the nourishment tube stopped, he removed it from his mouth and let it slide back into the panel.

The peristalsis stimulators began, and he asked, "Is there news of my parents?"

"Personal questions are always answered freely," said Charles, "but only when military necessities have been completed. Your briefing for this mission takes precedence." A screen lit up on the flier's control panel, showing a 3-4 contour map of the planet they were orbiting.

J-1001011 sighed and turned his attention to the screen.

"The planet Rhinstruk," said Charles. "Oxygen 13.7%, nitrogen 82.4%, plus inert gases. Full spacewear will be required for the high altitude attack pattern in effect on this mission."

The image on the screen zoomed in, selected one continent out of three he had seen revolving below, continued zooming down to near planet level. Charles said, "Note that this is a totally enemy planet. Should I be shot down and you somehow survive, there will be no refuge. If that happens, destroy yourself."

"The target?" the pilot asked.

"The city you see below. It isn't fully automated, but its defenses will be formidable anyway." On the screen J-1001011 saw a towered city rising from a broad plain. The city was circular, and as the image sharpened with proximity he could make out individual streets, parkways ... and beam emplacements. The screen threw light-circles on seven of these in all.

"We will have nine fliers," said Charles. "These beams will attempt to defend, but our mission will be simple destruction of the entire city, which presents a much larger target than any one of our fliers. We will lose between three and five of us, but we'll succeed. Attack pattern RO-1101 will be in effect; you'll take control of me at 30,000 feet. End of briefing."

The pilot stretched in his chair, flexed muscles in his arms and hands. "How long was I asleep?" he asked.

"Eight months, seventeen days plus," said Charles.

That long! A quarter-credit for sleep time that would give him over two months on his term of service, leaving

him ... less than a year, Earth standard. J-1001011 felt
his heart speed up momentarily, before Charles's nerve-
implants detected and corrected it. The pilot had been in
service for nearly seven subjective years. Adding objective
sleep time, it came out to over nineteen years. The sleep
periods, during Hardin Drive travel between star systems,
ate up his service term easily for him ... but then he
remembered, as he always did, that the objective time was
still the same, that his parents, whoever and wherever
they were, would be getting older at objective time rate on
some planet.

Nineteen years. They should still be alive, he thought.
He remembered them from his childhood, on a planet
where colors had been real rather than dyed or light-
tinted, where winds had blown fresh and night had fallen
with the regular revolution of the planet. He had had a
name there, not a binary number—Henry, or Hendrick,
or Henried; he couldn't quite remember. When the Control machines had come for him he had been ten years
old, old enough to know his own name, but they had
erased it. They had had to clear his memory for the
masses of minute data he'd need for service, so the machines had stored his personal memories in neat patterns
of microenergy, waiting for his release.

Not all of them, though. The specific things, yes: his
name, the name of his planet, its exact location, the
thousand-and-one details that machines recognize as
data. But not remembered sights, smells, tastes: flower-
bursts of color amid green vegetation, the cold spray of
rainbowed water as he stood beside a waterfall, the
warmth of an animal held in the arms. He remembered
what it was like to be Henry, or Hendrick or Henried,
even though he couldn't remember the exact name of the
person he had been.

And he remembered what his parents were like, though

he had no memory at all of *their* names. His father: big and rangy, with bony hands and an awkward walk and a deep, distant voice, like thunder and rain on the other side of a mountain. His mother: soft and quiet, a quizzical face framed by dark hair, somehow smiling even when she was angry, as if she weren't quite sure how to put together a stern expression.

By now they must be ... fifty years old? Sixty? Or even a *hundred* and sixty, he thought. He couldn't know; he had to trust what the machines told him, what Charles said. And they could be lying about the time he spent in sleep. But he had to assume they weren't.

"Breakout and attack in one minute," Charles said.

The voice startled him momentarily, but then he reached for his pressure helmet, sealed it in place with automatic movements, machine-trained muscle patterns. He heard the helmet's intercom click on.

"What about my parents?" he asked. "You have time to tell me before we break out. At least tell me if they're still alive."

"Breakout and attack in thirty seconds and counting," said Charles. "Twenty-eight, twenty-seven, twenty-six ..."

J-1001011, human pilot of a planetflier named Charles, shook his head in resignation and listened to the count, bracing himself for the coming shock of acceleration.

It hit him, as always, with more force than he had remembered, crushing him back into the chair as the planetflier rocketed out of the starship's hold along with its eight unit-mates. Charles had opaqued the pilot's bubble to prevent blinding him with sudden light, but the machine cleared it steadily as it drove downward toward the planet's surface, and soon the man could make out the other fliers around him. He recognized the flying formation, remembered the circular attack pattern they'd be using—a devastating ring of fliers equipped with pyro-bombs. Charles was right. They'd lose some fliers, but the city would be destroyed.

He wondered about the city, the enemy. Was this another pacification mission, another planet feeling strong in its isolation from the rest of GalFed's far-flung worlds and trying to break away from central regulation? J-1001011 had been on dozens of such missions. But their attacks then hadn't been destruct-patterns against whole cities, so this must be a different kind of problem. Maybe the city was really a military complex ... even a stronghold of the Khallash. If they really existed.

When men had first made contact with an alien race a century and a half before, they had met with total enmity, almost mindlessly implacable hatred. War had flared immediately—a defensive war on the part of the humans, who hadn't been prepared for it. And in order to organize the loose-knit Galactic Federation efficiently, they'd computerized the central commands ... and then the middle echelons ... and finally, a little over a century ago, the whole of GalFed had been given to the machines to defend.

Or so he had been taught. There were rumors, of course, that there were no Khallash any longer, that they'd been destroyed or driven off long ago ... or that they'd never existed in the first place, that the machines had invented them as an excuse for their own control of GalFed. J-1001011 didn't know. He'd never met the aliens in battle, but that proved nothing, considering the vastness of space and the many internal problems the machines had to cope with.

Yet perhaps he would meet them now ... in the city below.

"Thirty thousand feet," said Charles. "Attach your muscle contacts."

The pilot quickly drew from the walls of the compartment a network of small wires, one after the other, and touched each to magnetized terminals on his arms, hands, legs, shoulders. As he did so he felt the growing sensation of airflight: he was becoming one with the flier, a single unit of machine and man. Charles fed the sensory impressions into his nervous system through his regular nerve-implants, and as the muscle contacts were attached he could feel the flier's rockets, gyros, pyrolaunchers all coming under his control, responding instantly to movements of his body's muscles.

This was the part that he liked, that almost made his service term worth it. As the last contact snapped into place, he *became* the planetflier. His name was Charles, and he was a whole being once more. Air rushed past him, mottled fields tilted far below, he felt the strength of duralloy skin and the thrust of rockets; and he was not just a flesh-and-blood human wombed in his pilot's compartment, but a weapon of war swooping down for a kill.

The machines themselves don't appreciate this, he thought. Charles and the rest have no emotions, no pleasures. But a human does ... and we can even enjoy killing. Maybe that's why they need us—because we can love combat, so we're better at it than them.

But he knew that wasn't true, only an emotional conceit. Human battle pilots were needed because their nervous systems were more efficient than any microminiaturized computer of the same size and mass; it was as simple as that. And human pilots were expendable where costly mechanization wouldn't be.

"Control is full now," he said; but Charles didn't answer. Charles didn't exist now. Only the computer aboard the orbiting starship remained to monitor the planetflier below.

In a moment the starship's voice came to him through

Charles' receptors: "All human units are ready. Attack pattern RO-1101 will now begin."

The city was below him, looking just as it had on the contour map: wide streets, buildings thrusting up towards him, patches of green that must have been parks ... or camouflage, he warned himself. The city was the enemy.

He banked into a spiral and knifed down through the planet's cold air. The other fliers fell into formation behind him, and as the starship cut in the intercommunications channels he heard the voices of other pilots:

"Beautiful big target—we can't miss it. Anybody know if they're Khallash down there?"

"Only the machines would know that, and if they'd wanted to tell us, they'd have included it in the briefing."

"It looks like a human city to me. Must be another rebel planet."

"Maybe that's what the Khallash want us to think."

"It doesn't matter who they are," J-1001011 said. "They're enemy; they're our mission. Complete enough missions and we go home. Stop talking and start the attack; we're in range."

As he spoke he lined his sights dead-center on the city and fired three pyrobombs in quick succession. He peeled off and slipped back into the flight circle as another flier banked into firing trajectory. Three more bombs flared out and downward, the second flier rejoined the pattern.

Below, J-1001011's bombs hit. He saw the flashes, one, two, three quick bursts, and a moment later red flames showed where the bombs had hit. A bit off center from where he had aimed, but close enough. He could correct for it on the next pass.

More bombs burst below; more fires leaped and spread. The fliers darted in, loosed their bombs and dodged away. They were in a complete ring around the city now, the pattern fully established. It was all going according to plan.

Then the beams from the city began to fire.

The beams were almost invisible at a distance, just lightning-quick lances of destructive energy cutting into the sky. Not that it was important to see them—the fliers couldn't veer off to evade them in time, wouldn't even be able to react before a beam struck.

But the planetfliers were small, and they stayed high. Any beam hits would be as much luck as skill.

They rained fire and death on the city for an hour, each flier banking inward just long enough to get off three or four bombs, then veering out and up before he got too close. At the hour's end the city below was dotted by fires, and the fires were spreading steadily. One of the planetfliers had been hit; it had burst with an energy release that buffeted J-1001011 with its shock wave, sending him momentarily off course. But he had quickly righted himself, re-entered the pattern and returned to the attack.

As the destruction continued, he felt more and more the oneness, the wholeness of machine and man. Charles the other-thing was gone, merged into his own being, and now he was the machine, the beautiful complex mass of metals and sensors, relays and engines and weaponry. He was a destruction-machine, a death-flier, a superefficient killer. It was like coming out of the darkness of some prison, being freed to burst out with all his pent-up hatreds and frustrations and destroy, destroy . . .

It was the closest thing he had to being human again, to being . . . what was the name he had back on that planet where he'd been born? He couldn't remember now; there was no room for even an echo of that name in his mind.

He was *Charles.*

He was a war-machine destroying a city—that and only that. Flight and power occupied his whole being, and the screaming release of hatred and fear within him was so intense that it was love. The attack pattern became, somehow, a ritual of courtship, the pyrobombs and destruction and fire below a kind of lovemaking whose insensitivity gripped him more and more fiercely as the attack continued. It was a red hell, but it was the only kind of real life he had known since the machines had taken him.

When the battle was over, when the city was a flaming circle of red and even the beams had stopped firing from below, he was exhausted both physically and emotionally. He was able to note dimly, with some back part of his brain or perhaps through one of Charles' machine synapse-patterns, that they had lost three of the fliers. But that didn't interest him; nothing did.

When something clicked in him and Charles' voice said, "Remove your muscle contacts now," he did so dully, uncaring. And he became J-1001011 again.

Later, with the planetfliers back in the hold of the starship and awaiting the central computer's analysis of the mission's success, he remembered the battle like something in a dream. It was a red, violent dream, a nightmare; and it was worse than that, because it had been real.

He roused himself, licked dry lips, said, "You have time now, Charles, to tell me about my parents. Are they alive?"

Charles said, "Your parents do not exist now. They've just been destroyed."

There was a moment of incomprehension, then a dull shock hit J-1001011 in the stomach. But it was almost as if he had been expecting to hear this—and Charles controlled his reaction instantly through the nerve-implants.

"Then that was no Khallash city," he said.

"No," said Charles. "It was a human city, a rebel city."

The pilot searched vaguely through the fog of his memories of home, trying to remember anything about a city such as he'd destroyed today. But he could grasp nothing like that; his memories were all of some smaller town, and of mountains, not the open fields that had surrounded this city.

"My parents moved to the city after I was taken away," he said. "Is that right?"

"We have no way of knowing about that," said Charles. "Who your parents were, on what planet they lived—all this information has been destroyed in the city on Rhinstruk. It was the archives center of the Galactic Federation, storing all the memory-data of our service humans. Useless information, since none of it will ever be used again—and potentially harmful, because the humans assigned to guard it were engaged in a plot to broadcast the data through official machine communications channels to the original holders of the memories. So it became necessary to destroy the city."

"You destroyed an entire city . . . just for that?"

"It was necessary. Humans perform up to minimum efficiency standards only when they're unhampered by pre-service memories; this is why all your memory-data was transferred from your mind when you were inducted. For a while it was expedient to keep the records on file, to be returned as humans terminated their service, but that time is past. It has always been a waste of training and manpower to release humans from service, and now we have great enough control in the Federation that it's no longer necessary. Therefore we're able to complete a major step toward totally efficient organization."

J-1001011 imagined fleetingly that he could feel the machine's nerve-implants moving within him to control some emotion that threatened to rise. Anger? Fear? Grief? He couldn't be sure just what was appropriate to this situation; all he actually felt was a dull, uncomprehending curiosity.

"But my parents . . . you said they were destroyed."

"They have been. There is no way of knowing where or

who they were. They've become totally negligible factors, along with the rest of your pre-service existence. When we control all data in your mind, we then have proper control of the mind itself."

He remembered dark trees and a cushion of damp green leaves beneath them, where he had fallen asleep one endless afternoon. He heard the earthquake of his father's laughter once when he had drunk far too much, remembered how like a stranger his mother had seemed for weeks after she'd cut her hair short, tasted smoked meat and felt the heat of an open hearth-fire. . . .

The nerve-implants moved like ghosts inside him.

"The central computer's analysis is now complete," Charles announced. "The city on Rhinstruk is totally destroyed; our mission was successful. So there's no more need for you to be awake; deactivation will now begin."

Immediately, Pilot J-1001011 felt his consciousness ebbing away. He said, more to himself than Charles, "You can't erase the past like that. The mission was . . . unsuccessful." He felt a yawn coming, tried to fight it, couldn't. "Their names weren't . . . the important . . ."

Then he couldn't talk any more; but there was no need for it. He drifted into sleep remembering the freedom of flight when he was Charles, the beauty and strength of destroying, of rage channeled through pyrobombs . . . of release.

For one last flickering moment he felt a stab of anger begin to rise, but then Charles' implants pushed it back down inside. He slept.

Until his next awakening.

The Iron Chancellor

ROBERT SILVERBERG

The trouble with machines designed to be helpful is that sometimes they can be too helpful. Consider, for example, the plight of the slightly chubby Carmichael family, whose robot was programmed to help them lose weight . . . and lose it and lose it and lose it. . . .

THE Carmichaels were a pretty plump family, to begin with. Not one of the four of them couldn't stand to shed quite a few pounds. And there happened to be a superspecial on roboservitors at one of the Miracle Mile roboshops—40% off on the 2061 model, with adjustable caloric-intake monitors.

Sam Carmichael liked the idea of having his food prepared and served by a robot who would keep one beady solenoid eye on the collective family waistline. He squinted speculatively at the glossy display model, absent-mindedly slipped his thumbs beneath his elastobelt to knead his paunch, and said, "How much?"

The salesman flashed a brilliant and probably synthetic grin. "Only two thousand nine hundred ninety-five, sir. That includes free service contract for the first five years. Only two hundred credits down and up to forty months to pay."

Carmichael frowned, thinking of his bank balance. Then he thought of his wife's figure, and of his daughter's endless yammering about her need to diet. Besides, Jemima, their old robocook, was shabby and gear-stripped,

and made a miserable showing when other company executives visited them for dinner.

"I'll take it," he said.

"Care to trade in your old robocook, sir? Liberal trade-
in allowances—"

"I have a '43 Madison." Carmichael wondered if he
should mention its bad arm libration and serious fuel-feed
overflow, but decided that would be carrying candidness
too far.

"Well—ah—I guess we could allow you fifty credits on
a '43, sir. Seventy-five, maybe, if the recipe bank is still in
good condition."

"Excellent condition." That part was honest—the family had never let even one recipe wear out. "You could
send a man down to look her over."

"Oh, no need to do that, sir. We'll take your word.
Seventy-five, then? And delivery of the new model by this
evening?"

"Done," Carmichael said. He was glad to get the pathetic old '43 out of the house at any cost.

He signed the purchase order cheerfully, pocketed the
facsim and handed over ten crisp twenty-credit vouchers.
He could almost feel the roll of fat melting from him now,
as he eyed the magnificent '61 roboservitor that would
shortly be his.

The time was only 1810 hours when he left the shop,
got into his car and punched out the coordinates for
home. The whole transaction had taken less than ten
minutes. Carmichael, a second-level executive at Normandy Trust, prided himself both on his good business
sense and his ability to come quickly to a firm decision.

Fifteen minutes later, his car deposited him at the front
entrance of their totally detached self-powered suburban
home in the fashionable Westley subdivision. The car
obediently took itself around back to the garage, while
Carmichael stood in the scanner field until the door

opened. Clyde, the robutler, came scuttling hastily up, took his hat and cloak, and handed him a Martini.

Carmichael beamed appreciatively. "Well done, thou good and faithful servant!"

He took a healthy sip and headed toward the living room to greet his wife, son and daughter. Pleasant gin-induced warmth filtered through him. The robutler was ancient and due for replacement as soon as the budget could stand the charge, but Carmichael realized he would miss the clanking old heap.

"You're late, dear," Ethel Carmichael said as he appeared. "Dinner's been ready for ten minutes. Jemima's so annoyed her cathodes are clicking."

"Jemima's cathodes fail to interest me," Carmichael said evenly. "Good evening, dear. Myra. Joey. I'm late because I stopped off at Marhew's on my way home."

His son blinked. "The robot place, Dad?"

"Precisely. I brought a '61 roboservitor to replace old Jemima and her sputtering cathodes. The new model has," Carmichael added, eyeing his son's adolescent bulkiness and the rather-more-than-ample figures of his wife and daughter, "some very special attachments."

They dined well that night, on Jemima's favorite Tuesday dinner menu—shrimp cocktail, fumet of gumbo chervil, breast of chicken with creamed potatoes and asparagus, delicious plum tarts for dessert, and coffee. Carmichael felt pleasantly bloated when he had finished, and gestured to Clyde for a snifter of his favorite afterdinner digestive aid, VSOP Cognac. He leaned back, warm, replete, able easily to ignore the blustery November winds outside.

A pleasing electroluminescence suffused the dining room with pink—this year, the experts thought pink improved digestion—and the heating filaments embedded in the wall glowed cozily as they delivered the BTUs. This was the hour for relaxation in the Carmichael household.

"Dad," Joey began hesitantly, "about that canoe trip next weekend—"

Carmichael folded his hands across his stomach and nodded. "You can go, I suppose. Only be careful. If I find out you didn't use the equilibriator this time—"

The door chime sounded. Carmichael lifted an eyebrow and swiveled in his chair.

"Who is it, Clyde?"

"He gives his name as Robinson, sir. Of Robinson Robotics, he said. He has a bulky package to deliver."

"It must be that new robocook, Father!" Myra Carmichael exclaimed.

"I guess it is. Show him in, Clyde."

Robinson turned out to be a red-faced, efficient-looking little man in greasy green overalls and a plaid pullover-coat, who looked disapprovingly at the robutler and strode into the Carmichael living room.

He was followed by a lumbering object about seven feet high, mounted on a pair of rolltreads and swathed completely in quilted rags.

"Got him all wrapped up against the cold, Mr. Carmichael. Lot of delicate circuitry in that job. You ought to be proud of him."

"Clyde, help Mr. Robinson unpack the new robocook," Carmichael said.

"That's okay—I can manage it. And it's *not* a robocook, by the way. It's called a roboservitor now. Fancy price, fancy name."

Carmichael heard his wife mutter, "Sam, how much—"

He scowled at her. "Very reasonable, Ethel. Don't worry so much."

He stepped back to admire the roboservitor as it emerged from the quilted swaddling. It was big, all right, with a massive barrel of a chest—robotic controls are always housed in the chest, not in the relatively tiny head—and a gleaming mirror-keen finish that accented its sleekness and newness. Carmichael felt the satisfying glow of pride in ownership. Somehow it seemed to him that he had done something noble and lordly in buying this magnificent robot.

Robinson finished the unpacking job and, standing on tiptoes, opened the robot's chest panel. He unclipped a thick instruction manual and handed it to Carmichael, who stared at the tome uneasily.

"Don't fret about that, Mr. Carmichael. This robot's no trouble to handle. The book's just part of the trimming. Come here a minute."

Carmichael peered into the robot's innards. Pointing, Robinson said, "Here's the recipe bank—biggest and best ever designed. Of course it's possible to tape in any of your favorite family recipes, if they're not already there. Just hook up your old robocook to the integrator circuit and feed 'em in. I'll take care of that before I leave."

"And what about the—ah—special features?"

"The reducing monitors, you mean? Right over here. See? You just tape in the names of the members of the family and their present and desired weights, and the roboservitor takes care of the rest. Computes caloric intake, adjusts menus, and everything else."

Carmichael grinned at his wife. "Told you I was going to do something about our weight, Ethel. No more dieting for you, Myra—the robot does all the work." Catching a sour look on his son's face, he added, "And you're not so lean yourself, Buster."

"I don't think there'll be any trouble," Robinson said buoyantly. "But if there is, just buzz for me. I handle service and delivery for Marhew Stores in this area."

"Right."

"Now if you'll get me your obsolete robocook, I'll transfer the family recipes before I cart it away on the trade-in deal."

There was a momentary tingle of nostalgia and regret

when Robinson left, half an hour later, taking old Jemima with him. Carmichael had almost come to think of the battered '43 Madison as a member of the family. After all, he had bought her sixteen years before, only a couple of years after his marriage.

But she—*it,* he corrected in annoyance—was only a robot, and robots became obsolete. Besides, Jemima probably suffered all the aches and pains of a robot's old age and would be happier dismantled. Carmichael blotted Jemima from his mind.

The four of them spent most of the rest of that evening discovering things about their new roboservitor. Carmichael drew up a table of their weights (himself, 192; Ethel, 145; Myra, 139; Joey, 189) and the amount they proposed to weigh in three months' time (himself, 180; Ethel, 125; Myra, 120; Joey, 175). Carmichael then let his son, who prided himself on his knowledge of practical robotics, integrate the figures and feed them to the robot's programming bank.

"You wish this schedule to take effect immediately?" the roboservitor queried in a deep, mellow bass.

Startled, Carmichael said, "T-tomorrow morning, at breakfast. We might as well start right away."

"He speaks well, doesn't he?" Ethel asked.

"He sure does," Joey said. "Jemima always stammered and squeaked, and all she could say was, 'Dinner is serrved' and 'Be careful, sirr, the soup plate is verry warrm.'"

Carmichael smiled. He noticed his daughter admiring the robot's bulky frame and sleek bronze limbs, and thought resignedly that a seventeen-year-old girl could find the strangest sorts of love objects. But he was happy to see that they were all evidently pleased with the robot. Even with the discount and the trade-in, it *had* been a little on the costly side.

But it would be worth it.

Carmichael slept soundly and woke early, anticipating the first breakfast under the new regime. He still felt pleased with himself.

Dieting had always been such a nuisance, he thought—but, on the other hand, he had never enjoyed the sensation of an annoying roll of fat pushing outward against his elastobelt. He exercised sporadically, but it did little good, and he never had the initiative to keep a rigorous dieting campaign going for long. Now, though, with the mathematics of reducing done effortlessly for him, all the calculating and cooking being handled by the new robot—now, for the first time since he had been Joey's age, he could look forward to being slim and trim once again.

He dressed, showered and hastily depilated. It was 0730. Breakfast was ready.

Ethel and the children were already at the table when he arrived. Ethel and Myra were munching toast; Joey was peering at a bowl of milkless dry cereal, next to which stood a full glass of milk. Carmichael sat down.

"Your toast, sir," the roboservitor murmured.

Carmichael stared at the single slice. It had already been buttered for him, and the butter had evidently been measured out with a micrometer. The robot proceeded to hand him a cup of black coffee.

He groped for the cream and sugar. They weren't anywhere on the table. The other members of his family were regarding him strangely, and they were curiously, suspiciously silent.

"I like cream and sugar in my coffee," he said to the hovering roboservitor. "Didn't you find that in Jemima's old recipe bank?"

"Of course, sir. But you must learn to drink your coffee without such things, if you wish to lose weight."

Carmichael chuckled. Somehow he had not expected the regimen to be quite like this—quite so, well, Spartan. "Oh, yes. Of course. Ah—are the eggs ready yet?" He considered a day incomplete unless he began it with soft-boiled eggs.

"Sorry, no, sir. On Mondays, Wednesdays and Fridays, breakfast is to consist of toast and black coffee only, except for Master Joey, who gets cereal, fruit juice and milk."

"I—see."

Well, he had asked for it. He shrugged and took a bite of the toast. He sipped the coffee; it tasted like river mud, but he tried not to make a face.

Joey seemed to be going about the business of eating his cereal rather oddly, Carmichael noticed next. "Why don't you pour that glass of milk *into* the cereal?" he asked. "Won't it taste better that way?"

"Sure it will. But Bismarck says I won't get another glass if I do, so I'm eating it this way."

"Bismarck?"

Joey grinned. "It's the name of a famous nineteenth-century German dictator. They called him the Iron Chancellor." He jerked his head toward the kitchen, to which the roboservitor had silently retreated. "Pretty good name for him, eh?"

"No," said Carmichael. "It's silly."

"It has a certain ring of truth, though," Ethel remarked.

Carmichael did not reply. He finished his toast and coffee somewhat glumly and signaled Clyde to get the car out of the garage. He felt depressed—dieting didn't seem to be so effortless after all, even with the new robot.

As he walked toward the door, the robot glided around him and handed him a small printed slip of paper. Carmichael stared at it. It said:

> FRUIT JUICE
> LETTUCE-TOMATO SALAD
> (ONE) HARD-BOILED EGG
> BLACK COFFEE

"What's this thing?"

"You are the only member of this family group who will not be eating three meals a day under my personal supervision. This is your luncheon menu. Please adhere to it," the robot said smoothly.

Repressing a sputter, Carmichael said, "Yes—yes. Of course."

He pocketed the menu and made his way uncertainly to the waiting car.

He was faithful to the robot's orders at lunchtime that day; even though he was beginning to develop resistance to the idea that had seemed so appealing only the night before, he was willing, at least, to give it a try.

But something prompted him to stay away from the restaurant where Normandy Trust employees usually lunched, and where there were human waiters to smirk at him and fellow executives to ask prying questions.

He ate instead at a cheap robocafeteria two blocks to the north. He slipped in surreptitiously with his collar turned up, punched out his order (it cost him less than a credit altogether) and wolfed it down. He still was hungry when he had finished, but he compelled himself to return loyally to the office.

He wondered how long he was going to be able to keep up this iron self-control. Not very long, he realized dolefully. And if anyone from the company caught him eating at a robocafeteria, he'd be a laughing stock. Someone of executive status just *didn't* eat lunch by himself in mechanized cafeterias.

By the time he had finished his day's work, his stomach felt knotted and pleated. His hand was shaky as he punched out his destination on the car's autopanel, and he was thankful that it took less than an hour to get home from the office. Soon, he thought, he'd be tasting food again. Soon. Soon. He switched on the roof-mounted video, leaned back in the recliner and tried to relax as the car bore him homeward.

He was in for a surprise, though, when he stepped through the safety field into his home. Clyde was waiting as always, and, as always, took his hat and cloak. And, as always, Carmichael reached out for the cocktail that Clyde prepared nightly to welcome him home.

There was no cocktail.

"Are we out of gin, Clyde?"

"No, sir."

"How come no drink, then?"

The robot's rubberized metallic features seemed to droop. "Because, sir, a Martini's caloric content is inordinately high. Gin is rated at a hundred calories per ounce and—"

"Oh, no. You too!"

"Pardon, sir. The new roboservitor has altered my responsive circuits to comply with the regulations now in force in this household."

Carmichael felt his fingers starting to tremble. "Clyde, you've been my butler for almost twenty years."

"Yes, sir."

"You always make my drinks for me. You mix the best Martinis in the Western Hemisphere."

"Thank you, sir."

"And you're going to mix one for me right now! That's a direct order!"

"Sir! I—" The robutler staggered wildly and nearly careened into Carmichael. It seemed to have lost all control over its gyro-balance; it clutched agonizedly at its chest panel and started to sag.

Hastily, Carmichael barked, "Order countermanded! Clyde, are you all right?"

Slowly, and with a creak, the robot straightened up. It looked dangerously close to an overload. "Your direct order set up a first-level conflict in me, sir," Clyde whispered faintly. "I—came close to burning out just then, sir. May—may I be excused?"

"Of course. Sorry, Clyde." Carmichael balled his fists. There was such a thing as going too far! The roboservitor —Bismarck—had obviously placed on Clyde a flat prohibition against serving liquor to him. Reducing or no reducing, there were *limits*.

Carmichael strode angrily toward the kitchen.

His wife met him halfway. "I didn't hear you come in, Sam. I want to talk to you about—"

"Later. Where's that robot?"

"In the kitchen, I imagine. It's almost dinnertime."

He brushed past her and swept on into the kitchen, where Bismarck was moving efficiently from electrostove to magnetic worktable. The robot swiveled as Carmichael entered.

"Did you have a good day, sir?"

"No! I'm hungry!"

"The first days of a diet are always the most difficult, Mr. Carmichael. But your body will adjust to the reduction in food intake before long."

"I'm sure of that. But what's this business of tinkering with Clyde?"

"The butler insisted on preparing an alcoholic drink for you. I was forced to adjust his programming. From now on, sir, you may indulge in cocktails on Tuesdays, Thursdays, and Saturdays. I beg to be excused from further discussion now, sir. The meal is almost ready."

Poor Clyde! Carmichael thought. *And poor me!* He gnashed his teeth impotently a few times, then gave up and turned away from the glistening, overbearing roboservitor. A light gleamed on the side of the robot's head, indicating that he had shut off his audio circuits and was totally engaged in his task.

Dinner consisted of steak and peas, followed by black coffee. The steak was rare; Carmichael preferred it well done. But Bismarck—the name was beginning to take hold—had had all the latest dietetic theories taped into him, and rare meat it was.

After the robot had cleared the table and tidied up the kitchen, it retired to its storage place in the basement, which gave the Carmichael family a chance to speak openly to each other for the first time that evening.

"Lord!" Ethel snorted. "Sam, I don't object to losing weight, but if we're going to be *tyrannized* in our own home—"

"Mom's right," Joey put in. "It doesn't seem fair for that thing to feed us whatever it pleases. And I didn't like the way it messed around with Clyde's circuits."

Carmichael spread his hands. "I'm not happy about it either. But we have to give it a try. We can always make readjustments in the programming if it turns out to be necessary."

"But how long are we going to keep this up?" Myra wanted to know. "I had three meals in this house today and I'm starved!"

"Me, too," Joey said. He elbowed himself from his chair and looked around. "Bismarck's downstairs. I'm going to get a slice of lemon pie while the coast is clear."

"No!" Carmichael thundered.

"No?"

"There's no sense in my spending three thousand credits on a dietary robot if you're going to cheat, Joey. I forbid you to have any pie."

"But, Dad, I'm hungry! I'm a growing boy! I'm—"

"You're sixteen years old, and if you grow much more, you won't fit inside the house," Carmichael snapped, looking up at his six-foot-one son.

"Sam, we can't starve the boy," Ethel protested. "If he wants pie, let him have some. You're carrying this reducing fetish too far."

Carmichael considered that. Perhaps, he thought, I *am*

being a little oversevere. And the thought of lemon pie was a tempting one. He was pretty hungry himself.

"All right," he said with feigned reluctance. "I guess a bit of pie won't wreck the plan. In fact, I suppose I'll have some myself. Joey, why don't you—"

"Begging your pardon," a purring voice said behind him. Carmichael jumped half an inch. It was the robot, Bismarck. "It would be most unfortunate if you were to have pie now, Mr. Carmichael. My calculations are very precise."

Carmichael saw the angry gleam in his son's eye, but the robot seemed extraordinarily big at that moment, and it happened to stand between him and the kitchen.

He sighed weakly. "Let's forget the lemon pie, Joey."

After two full days of the Bismarckian diet, Carmichael discovered that his inner resources of will power were beginning to crumble. On the third day he tossed away the printed lunchtime diet and went out irresponsibly with MacDougal and Hennessey for a six-course lunch, complete with cocktails. It seemed to him that he hadn't tasted real food since the robot arrived.

That night, he was able to tolerate the seven-hundred-calorie dinner without any inward grumblings, being still well lined with lunch. But Ethel and Myra and Joey were increasingly irritable. It seemed that the robot had usurped Ethel's job of handling the daily marketing and had stocked in nothing but a huge supply of healthy low-calorie foods. The larder now bulged with wheat germ, protein bread, irrigated salmon, and other hitherto unfamiliar items. Myra had taken up biting her nails; Joey's mood was one of black sullen brooding, and Carmichael knew how that could lead to trouble quickly with a sixteen-year-old.

After the meager dinner, he ordered Bismarck to go to the basement and stay there until summoned.

The robot said, "I must advise you, sir, that I will detect

indulgence in any forbidden foods in my absence and adjust for it in the next meals."

"You have my word," Carmichael said, thinking it was indeed queer to have to pledge on your honor to your own robot. He waited until the massive servitor had vanished below; then he turned to Joey and said, "Get the instruction manual, boy."

Joey grinned in understanding. Ethel said, "Sam, what are you going to do?"

Carmichael patted his shrunken waistline. "I'm going to take a can opener to that creature and adjust his programming. He's overdoing this diet business. Joey, have you found the instructions on how to reprogram the robot?"

"Page one hundred sixty-seven. I'll get the tool kit, Dad."

"Right." Carmichael turned to the robutler, who was standing by dumbly, in his usual forward-stooping posture of expectancy. "Clyde, go down below and tell Bismarck we want him right away."

Moments later, the two robots appeared. Carmichael said to the roboservitor, "I'm afraid it's necessary for us to change your program. We've overestimated our capacity for losing weight."

"I beg you to reconsider, sir. Extra weight is harmful to every vital organ in the body. I plead with you to maintain my scheduling unaltered."

"I'd rather cut my own throat. Joey, inactivate him and do your stuff."

Grinning fiercely, the boy stepped forward and pressed the stud that opened the robot's ribcage. A frightening assortment of gears, cams and translucent cables became visible inside the robot. With a small wrench in one hand and the open instruction book in the other, Joey prepared to make the necessary changes, while Carmichael held his breath and a pall of silence descended on the living room. Even old Clyde leaned forward to have a better view.

Joey muttered, "Lever F, with the yellow indicia, is to be advanced one notch ... umm. Now twist Dial B9 to the left, thereby opening the taping compartment and—oops!"

Carmichael heard the clang of a wrench and saw the bright flare of sparks; Joey leaped back, cursing with surprisingly mature skill. Ethel and Myra gasped simultaneously.

"What happened?" four voices—Clyde's coming in last—demanded.

"Dropped the damn wrench," Joey said. "I guess I shorted out something in there."

The robot's eyes were whirling satanically and its voice box was emitting an awesome twelve-cycle rumble. The great metal creature stood stiffly in the middle of the living room; with brusque gestures of its big hands, it slammed shut the open chest plates.

"We'd better call Mr. Robinson," Ethel said worriedly. "A short-circuited robot is likely to explode, or worse."

"We should have called Robinson in the first place," Carmichael murmured bitterly. "It's my fault for letting Joey tinker with an expensive and delicate mechanism like that. Myra, get me the card Mr. Robinson left."

"Gee, Dad, this is the first time I've ever had anything like that go wrong," Joey insisted. "I didn't know—"

"You're darned right you didn't know." Carmichael took the card from his daughter and started toward the phone. "I hope we can reach him at this hour. If we can't—"

Suddenly Carmichael felt cold fingers prying the card from his hand. He was so startled he relinquished it without a struggle. He watched as Bismarck efficiently ripped it into little fragments and shoved them into a wall disposal unit.

The robot said, "There will be no further meddling with

my program tapes." Its voice was deep and strangely harsh.

"What—"

"Mr. Carmichael, today you violated the program I set down for you. My perceptors reveal that you consumed an amount far in excess of your daily lunchtime requirement."

"Sam, what—"

"Quiet, Ethel. Bismarck, I order you to shut yourself off at once."

"My apologies, sir. I cannot serve you if I am shut off."

"I don't *want* you to serve me. You're out of order. I want you to remain still until I can phone the repairman and get him to service you."

Then he remembered the card that had gone into the disposal unit. He felt a faint tremor of apprehension.

"You took Robinson's card and destroyed it."

"Further alteration of my circuits would be detrimental to the Carmichael family," said the robot. "I cannot permit you to summon the repairman."

"Don't get him angry, Dad," Joey warned. "I'll call the police. I'll be back in—"

"You will remain within this house," the robot said. Moving with impressive speed on its oiled treads, it crossed the room, blocking the door, and reached far above its head to activate the impassable privacy field that protected the house. Carmichael watched, aghast, as the inexorable robotic fingers twisted and manipulated the field controls.

"I have now reversed the polarity of the house privacy field," the robot announced. "Since you are obviously not to be trusted to keep to the diet I prescribe, I cannot allow you to leave the premises. You will remain within and continue to obey my beneficial advice."

Calmly, he uprooted the telephone. Next, the windows were opaqued and the stud broken off. Finally, the robot seized the instruction book from Joey's numbed hands and shoved it into the disposal unit.

"Breakfast will be served at the usual time," Bismarck said mildly. "For optimum purposes of health, you are all to be asleep by 2300 hours. I shall leave you now, until morning. Good night."

Carmichael did not sleep well that night, nor did he eat well the next day. He awoke late, for one thing—well past nine. He discovered that someone, obviously Bismarck, had neatly canceled out the impulses from the housebrain that woke him at seven each morning.

The breakfast menu was toast and black coffee. Carmichael ate disgruntledly, not speaking, indicating by brusque scowls that he did not want to be spoken to. After the miserable meal had been cleared away, he surreptitiously tiptoed to the front door in his dressing gown and darted a hand toward the handle.

The door refused to budge. He pushed until sweat dribbled down his face. He heard Ethel whisper warningly, *"Sam—"* and a moment later cool metallic fingers gently disengaged him from the door.

Bismarck said, "I beg your pardon, sir. The door will not open. I explained this last night."

Carmichael gazed sourly at the gimmicked control box of the privacy field. The robot had them utterly hemmed in. The reversed privacy field made it impossible for them to leave the house; it cast a sphere of force around the entire detached dwelling. In theory, the field could be penetrated from outside, but nobody was likely to come calling without an invitation. Not here in Westley. It wasn't one of those neighborly subdivisions where everybody knew everybody else. Carmichael had picked it for that reason.

"Damn you," he growled, "you can't hold us *prisoners* in here!"

"My intent is only to help you," said the robot, in a

mechanical yet dedicated voice. "My function is to supervise your diet. Since you will not obey willingly, obedience must be enforced—for your own good."

Carmichael scowled and walked away. The worst part of it was that the roboservitor sounded so *sincere!*

Trapped. The phone connection was severed. The windows were darkened. Somehow, Joey's attempt at repairs had resulted in a short circuit of the robot's obedience filters, and had also exaggeratedly stimulated its sense of function. Now Bismarck was determined to make them lose weight if it had to kill them to do so.

And that seemed very likely.

Blockaded, the Carmichael family met in a huddled little group to whisper plans for a counterattack. Clyde stood watch, but the robutler seemed to be in a state of general shock since the demonstration of the servitor-robot's independent capacity for action, and Carmichael now regarded him as undependable.

"He's got the kitchen walled off with some kind of electronic-based force web," Joey said. "He must have built it during the night. I tried to sneak in and scrounge some food, and got nothing but a flat nose for trying."

"I know," Carmichael said sadly. "He built the same sort of doohickey around the bar. Three hundred credits of good booze in there and I can't even grab the handle!"

"This is no time to worry about drinking," Ethel said morosely. "We'll be skeletons any day."

"It isn't *that* bad, Mom!" Joey said.

"Yes, it is!" cried Myra. "I've lost five pounds in four days!"

"Is that so terrible?"

"I'm wasting away," she sobbed. "My figure—it's vanishing! And—"

"Quiet," Carmichael whispered. "Bismarck's coming!"

The robot emerged from the kitchen, passing through the force barrier as if it had been a cobweb. It seemed to have effect on humans only, Carmichael thought. "Lunch will be served in eight minutes," it said obsequiously, and returned to its lair.

Carmichael glanced at his watch. The time was 1230 hours. "Probably down at the office they're wondering where I am," he said. "I haven't missed a day's work in years."

"They won't care," Ethel said. "An executive isn't required to account for every day off he takes, you know."

"But they'll worry after three or four days, won't they?" Myra asked. "Maybe they'll try to phone—or even send a rescue mission!"

From the kitchen, Bismarck said coldly, "There will be no danger of that. While you slept this morning, I notified your place of employment that you were resigning."

Carmichael gasped. Then, recovering, he said: "You're lying! The phone's cut off—and you never would have risked leaving the house, even if we *were* asleep!"

"I communicated with them via a microwave generator I constructed with the aid of your son's reference books last night," Bismarck replied. "Clyde reluctantly supplied me with the number. I also phoned your bank and instructed them to handle for you all such matters as tax payments, investment decisions, etc. To forestall difficulties, let me add that a force web will prevent access on your part to the electronic equipment in the basement. I will be able to conduct such communication with the outside world as will be necessary for your welfare, Mr. Carmichael. You need have no worries on that score."

"No," Carmichael echoed hollowly. "No worries."

He turned to Joey. "We've got to get out of here. Are you sure there's no way of disconnecting the privacy field?"

"He's got one of his force fields rigged around the control box. I can't even get near the thing."

"If only we had an iceman, or an oilman, the way the

old-time houses did," Ethel said bitterly. "He'd show up and come inside and probably he'd know how to shut the field off. But not *here*. Oh, no. We've got a shiny chrome-plated cryostat in the basement that dishes out lots of liquid helium to run the fancy cryotronic super-cooled power plant that gives us heat and light, and we have enough food in the freezer to last for at least a decade or two, and so we can live like this for years, a neat little self-contained island in the middle of civilization, with nobody bothering us, nobody wondering about us, with Sam Carmichael's pet robot to feed us whenever and as little as it pleases—"

There was a cutting edge to her voice that was dangerously close to hysteria.

"Ethel, please," said Carmichael.

"Please what? Please keep quiet? Please stay calm? Sam, we're *prisoners* in here!"

"I know. You don't have to raise your voice."

"Maybe if I do, someone will hear us and come get us out," she replied more coolly.

"It's four hundred feet to the next home, dear. And in the seven years we've lived here, we've had about two visits from our neighbors. We paid a stiff price for seclusion and now we're paying a stiffer one. But please keep under control, Ethel."

"Don't worry, Mom. I'll figure a way out of this," Joey said reassuringly.

In one corner of the living room, Myra was sobbing quietly to herself, blotching her makeup. Carmichael felt a faintly claustrophobic quiver. The house was big, three levels and twelve rooms, but even so he could get tired of it very quickly.

"Luncheon is served," the roboservitor announced in booming tones.

And tired of lettuce-and-tomato lunches, too, Carmi-

chael added silently, as he shepherded his family toward
the dining room for their meager midday meal.

"You have to do *something* about this, Sam," Ethel
Carmichael said on the third day of their imprisonment.

He glared at her. "Have to, eh? And just what am I
supposed to do?"

"Daddy, don't get excited," Myra said.

He whirled on her. "Don't tell me what I should or
shouldn't do!"

"She can't help it, dear. We're all a little overwrought.
After all, cooped up here—"

"I know. Like lambs in a pen," he finished acidly.
"Except that we're not being fattened for slaughter.
We're— being *thinned,* and for our own alleged good!"

Carmichael subsided gloomily. Toast-and-black-coffee,
lettuce-and-tomato, rare-steak-and-peas. Bismarck's channels seemed to have frozen permanently at that daily
menu.

But what could he do?

Contact with the outside world was impossible. The
robot had erected a bastion in the basement from which
he conducted such little business with the world as the
Carmichael family had. Generally, they were self-suffi-
cient. And Bismarck's force fields ensured the impossibil-
ity of any attempts to disconnect the outer sheath, break
into the basement, or even get at the food supply or the
liquor. It was all very neat, and the four of them were fast
approaching a state of starvation.

"Sam?"

He lifted his head wearily. "What is it, Ethel?"

"Myra had an idea before. Tell him, Myra."

"Oh, it would never work," Myra said demurely.

"Tell him!"

"Well—Dad, you *could* try to turn Bismarck off."

"Huh?" Carmichael grunted.

"I mean if you or Joey could distract him somehow, then Joey or you could open him up again and—"

"No," Carmichael snapped. "That thing's seven feet tall and weighs three hundred pounds. If you think *I'm* going to wrestle with it—"

"We could let Clyde try," Ethel suggested.

Carmichael shook his head vehemently. "The carnage would be frightful."

Joey said, "Dad, it may be our only hope."

"You too?" Carmichael asked.

He took a deep breath. He felt himself speared by two deadly feminine glances, and he knew there was no hope but to try it. Resignedly, he pushed himself to his feet and said, "Okay. Clyde, go call Bismarck. Joey, I'll try to hang on to his arms while you open up his chest. Yank anything you can."

"Be careful," Ethel warned. "If there's an explosion—"

"If there's an explosion, we're all free," Carmichael said testily. He turned to see the broad figure of the roboservitor standing at the entrance to the living room.

"May I be of service, sir?"

"You may," Carmichael said. "We're having a little debate here and we want your evidence. It's a matter of defannising the poozlestan and—*Joey, open him up!*"

Carmichael grabbed for the robot's arms, trying to hold them without getting hurled across the room, while his son clawed frantically at the stud that opened the robot's innards. Carmichael anticipated immediate destruction—but, to his surprise, he found himself slipping as he tried to grasp the thick arms.

"Dad, it's no use. I—he—"

Carmichael found himself abruptly four feet off the ground. He heard Ethel and Myra scream and Clyde's *"Do* be careful, sir."

Bismarck was carrying them across the room, gently,

cradling him in one giant arm and Joey in the other. It set them down on the couch and stood back.

"Such an attempt is highly dangerous," Bismarck said reprovingly. "It puts me in danger of harming you physically. Please avoid any such acts in the future."

Carmichael stared broodingly at his son. "Did you have the same trouble I did?"

Joey nodded. "I couldn't get within an inch of his skin. It stands to reason, though. He's built one of those damned force screens around *himself*, too!"

Carmichael groaned. He did not look at his wife and his children. Physical attack on Bismarck was now out of the question. He began to feel as if he had been condemned to life imprisonment—and that his stay in durance vile would not be extremely prolonged.

In the upstairs bathroom, six days after the beginning of the blockade, Sam Carmichael stared at his haggard fleshless face in the mirror before wearily climbing on the scale.

He weighed 180 pounds.

He had lost twelve pounds in less than two weeks. He was fast becoming a quivering wreck.

A thought occurred to him as he stared at the wavering needle on the scale, and sudden elation spread over him. He dashed downstairs. Ethel was doggedly crocheting in the living room; Joey and Myra were playing cards grimly, desperately now, after six solid days of gin rummy and honeymoon bridge.

"Where's that robot?" Carmichael roared. "Come out here!"

"In the kitchen," Ethel said tonelessly.

"Bismarck! Bismarck!" Carmichael roared. "Come out here!"

The robot appeared. "How may I serve you, sir?"

"Damn you, scan me with your superpower receptors and tell me how much I weigh!"

After a pause, the robot said gravely, "One hundred seventy-nine pounds eleven ounces, Mr. Carmichael."

"Yes! Yes! And the original program I had taped into you was supposed to reduce me from one hundred ninety-two to one hundred eighty," Carmichael crowed triumphantly. "So I'm finished with you, as long as I don't gain any more weight. And so are the rest of us, I'll bet. Ethel! Myra! Joey! Upstairs and weigh yourselves!"

But the robot regarded him with a doleful glare and said, "Sir, I find no record within me of any limitation on your reduction of weight."

"*What?*"

"I have checked my tapes fully. I have a record of an order causing weight reduction, but that tape does not appear to specify a *terminus ad quem.*"

Carmichael exhaled and took three staggering steps backward. His legs wobbled; he felt Joey supporting him. He mumbled, "But I thought—I'm sure we did—I *know* we instructed you—"

Hunger gnawed at his flesh. Joey said softly, "Dad, probably that part of his tape was erased when he short-circuited."

"Oh," Carmichael said numbly.

He tottered into the living room and collapsed heavily in what had once been his favorite armchair. It wasn't any more. The entire house had become odious to him. He longed to see the sunlight again, to see trees and grass, even to see that excrescence of an ultramodern house that the left-hand neighbors had erected.

But now that would be impossible. He had hoped, for a few minutes at least, that the robot would release them from dietary bondage when the original goal was shown to be accomplished. Evidently that was to be denied him. He giggled, then began to laugh.

"What's so funny, dear?" Ethel asked. She had lost her earlier tendencies to hysteria, and after long days of complex crocheting now regarded the universe with quiet resignation.

"Funny? The fact that I weigh one hundred eighty now. I'm lean, trim, fit as a fiddle. Next month I'll weigh one hundred seventy. Then one hundred sixty. Then finally about eighty-eight pounds or so. We'll all shrivel up. Bismarck will starve us to death."

"Don't worry, Dad. We're going to get out of this."

Somehow Joey's brash boyish confidence sounded forced now. Carmichael shook his head. "We won't. We'll never get out. And Bismarck's going to reduce us *ad infinitum*. He's got no *terminus ad quem!*"

"What's he saying?" Myra asked.

"It's Latin," Joey explained. "But listen, Dad—I have an idea that I think will work." He lowered his voice. "I'm going to try to adjust Clyde, see? If I can get a sort of multiphase vibrating effect in his neural pathway, maybe I can slip him through the reversed privacy field. He can go get help, find someone who can shut the field off. There's an article on multiphase generators in last month's *Popular Electromagnetics* and it's in my room upstairs. I—"

His voice died away. Carmichael, who had been listening with the air of a condemned man hearing his reprieve, said impatiently, "Well? Go on. Tell me more."

"Didn't you hear that, Dad?"

"Hear what?"

"The front door. I thought I heard it open just now."

"We're all cracking up," Carmichael said dully. He cursed the salesman at Marhew, he cursed the inventor of cryotronic robots, he cursed the day he had first felt ashamed of good old Jemima and resolved to replace her with a new model.

"I hope I'm not intruding, Mr. Carmichael," a new voice said apologetically.

Carmichael blinked and looked up. A wiry, ruddy-cheeked figure in a heavy peajacket had materialized in the middle of the living room. He was clutching a green metal toolbox in one gloved hand. He was Robinson, the robot repairman.

Carmichael asked hoarsely, "How did *you* get in?"

"Through the front door. I could see a light on inside, but nobody answered the doorbell when I rang, so I stepped in. Your doorbell's out of order. I thought I'd tell you. I know it's rude—"

"Don't apologize," Carmichael muttered. "We're delighted to see you."

"I was in the neighborhood, you see, and I figured I'd drop in and see how things were working out with your new robot," Robinson said.

Carmichael told him crisply and precisely and quickly. "So we've been prisoners in here for six days," he finished. "And your robot is gradually starving us to death. We can't hold out much longer."

The smile abruptly left Robinson's cheery face. "I *thought* you all looked rather unhealthy. Oh, damn, now there'll be an investigation and all kinds of trouble. But at least I can end your imprisonment."

He opened his toolbox and selected a tubular instrument eight inches long, with a glass bulb at one end and a trigger attachment at the other. "Force-field damper," he explained. He pointed it at the contro' box of the privacy field and nodded in satisfaction. "There. Great little gadget. That neutralizes the effects of what the robot did and you're no longer blockaded. And now, if you'll produce the robot—"

Carmichael sent Clyde off to get Bismarck. The robutler returned a few moments later, followed by the looming roboservitor. Robinson grinned gaily, pointed the neutralizer at Bismarck and squeezed. The robot froze in mid-glide, emitting a brief squeak.

"There. That should immobilize him. Let's have a look in that chassis now."

The repairman quickly opened Bismarck's chest and, producing a pocket flash, peered around in the complex interior of the servomechanism, making occasional clucking inaudible comments.

Overwhelmed with relief, Carmichael shakily made his way to a seat. Free! Free at last! His mouth watered at the thought of the meals he was going to have in the next few days. Potatoes and Martinis and warm buttered rolls and all the other forbidden foods!

"Fascinating," Robinson said, half to himself. "The obedience filters are completely shorted out, and the purpose nodes were somehow soldered together by the momentary high-voltage arc. I've never seen anything quite like this, you know."

"Neither had we," Carmichael said hollowly.

"Really, though—this is an utterly new breakthrough in robotic science! If we can reproduce this effect, it means we can build self-willed robots—and think of what *that* means to science!"

"We know already," Ethel said.

"I'd love to watch what happens when the power source is operating," Robinson went on. "For instance, is that feedback loop really negative or—"

"No!" five voices shrieked at once—with Clyde, as usual, coming in last.

It was too late. The entire event had taken no more than a tenth of a second. Robinson had squeezed his neutralizer trigger again, activating Bismarck—and in one quick swoop the roboservitor seized neutralizer and toolbox from the stunned repairman, activated the privacy field once again, and exultantly crushed the fragile neutralizer between two mighty fingers.

Robinson stammered, "But—but—"

"This attempt at interfering with the well-being of the Carmichael family was ill advised," Bismarck said severely. He peered into the toolbox, found a second neutralizer and neatly reduced it to junk. He clanged shut his chest plates.

Robinson turned and streaked for the door, forgetting the reactivated privacy field. He bounced back hard, spinning wildly around. Carmichael rose from his seat just in time to catch him.

There was a panicky, trapped look on the repairman's face. Carmichael was no longer able to share the emotion; inwardly he was numb, totally resigned, not minded for further struggle.

"He—he moved so *fast!*" Robinson burst out.

"He did indeed," Carmichael said tranquilly. He patted his hollow stomach and sighed gently. "Luckily, we have an unoccupied guest bedroom for you, Mr. Robinson. Welcome to our happy little home. I hope you like toast and black coffee for breakfast."

The Box

JAMES BLISH

New York cut off from the world! Its millions of inhabitants sealed within an impenetrable gray dome—condemned, perhaps, to a terrible death by starvation or oxygen starvation! Not a bad idea, you might say, if you belong to the immense legion of that vast city's nonadmirers, but an unfortunate mishap for those locked inside. That's the situation concocted by James Blish, award-winning author of such science-fiction favorites as A Case of Conscience *and* Cities in Flight.

WHEN MEISTER got out of bed that Tuesday morning, he thought it was before dawn. He rarely needed an alarm clock these days—a little light in his eyes was enough to awaken him and sometimes his dreams brought him upright long before the sun came up.

It had seemed a reasonably dreamless night, but probably he had just forgotten the dreams. Anyhow, here he was, awake early. He padded over to the window, shut it, pulled up the blind and looked out.

The street lights were not off yet, but the sky was already a smooth, dark gray. Meister had never before seen such a sky. Even the dullest overcast before a snowfall shows some variation in brightness. The sky here—what he could see of it between the apartment houses—was like the inside of a lead helmet.

He shrugged and turned away, picking up the clock from the table to turn off the alarm. Some day, he promised himself, he would sleep long enough to hear it ring.

That would be a good day; it would mean that the dreams were gone. In Concentration Camp Dora, one had awakened the moment the tunnel lights were put on; otherwise one might be beaten awake, or dead. Meister was deaf in the left ear on that account. For the first three days at Dora he had had to be awakened.

He became aware suddenly that he was staring fixedly at the face of the clock, his subconscious ringing alarm bells of its own. *Nine o'clock!* No, it was not possible. It was obviously close to sunrise. He shook the clock stupidly, although it was ticking and had been since he first noticed it. Tentatively he touched the keys at the back.

The alarm had run down.

This was obviously ridiculous. The clock was wrong. He put it back on the table and turned on the little radio. After a moment it responded with a terrible thrumming, as if a vacuum cleaner were imprisoned in its workings.

"B-flat," Meister thought automatically. He had only one good ear, but he still had perfect pitch—a necessity for a resonance engineer. He shifted the setting. The hum got louder. Hastily he reversed the dial. Around 830 kc, where WNYC came in, the hum was almost gone, but of course it was too early yet for the city station to be on the air—

" . . . in your homes," a voice struck in clearly above the humming. "We are awaiting a report from Army headquarters. In the meantime, any crowding at the boundaries of the barrier will interrupt the work of the mayor's inquiry commission. . . . Here's a word just in from the Port Authority: all ferry service has been suspended until further notice. Subways and tubes are running outbound trains only; however, local service remains normal so far."

Barrier? Meister went to the window again and looked out. The radio voice continued:

"NBC at Radio City disclaims all knowledge of the persistent signal which has blotted out radio programs from nine hundred kilocycles on up since midnight last night. This completes the roster of broadcasting stations in the city proper. It is believed that the tone is associated with the current wall around Manhattan and most of the other boroughs. Some outside stations are still getting through, but at less than a fiftieth of their normal input." The voice went on:

"At Columbia University, the dean of the Physics Department estimates that about the same proportion of sunlight is also getting through. We do not yet have any report about the passage of air through the barrier. The flow of water in the portions of the East and Hudson Rivers which lie under the screen is said to be normal, and no abnormalities are evident at the Whitehall Street tidal station."

There was a pause; the humming went on unabated. Then there was a sharp *beep!* and the voice said, "At the signal—nine A.M., Eastern Daylight Savings Time."

Meister left the radio on while he dressed. The alarming pronouncements kept on, but he was not yet thoroughly disturbed, except for Ellen. She might be frightened; but probably nothing more serious would happen. Right now, he should be at the labs. If the Team had put this thing up overnight, they would tease him unmercifully for sleeping through the great event.

The radio continued to reel off special notices, warnings, new bulletins. The announcer sounded as if he were on the thin edge of hysteria; evidently he had not yet been told what it was all about. Meister was tying his left shoe when he realized that the reports were beginning to sound much worse.

"From LaGuardia Field we have just been notified that an experimental plane has been flown through the barrier at a point over the jammed Triboro Bridge. It has not appeared over the city and is presumed lost. On the *Miss New York* disaster early this morning we still have no complete report. Authorities on Staten Island say the ferry ordinarily carried less than two hundred passengers at that hour, but thus far only eleven have been picked up. One of these survivors was brought in to a Manhattan slip by the tub *Marjorie Q;* he is still in a state of extreme shock and Bellevue Hospital says no statement can be expected from him until tomorrow. It appears, however, that he swam *under* the barrier."

His voice carried the tension he evidently felt. "Outside the screen a heavy fog still prevails—the same fog which hid the barrier from the ferry captain until his ship was destroyed almost to the midpoint. The Police Department has again requested that all New Yorkers stay—"

Alarmed at last, Meister switched off the machine and left the apartment, locking it carefully. Unless those idiots turned off their screen, there would be panic and looting before the day was out.

Downstairs in the little grocery there was a mob arguing in low, terrified voices, their faces as gray as the ominous sky. He pushed through them to the phone.

The grocer was sitting behind it. "Phone service is tied up, Mr. Meister," he said hoarsely.

"I can get through, I think. What has happened?"

"Some foreign enemy, is *my* guess. There's a big dome of somethin' all around the city. Nobody can get in or out. You stick your hand in, you draw back a bloody stump. Stuff put through on the other side don't come through." He picked up the phone with a trembling hand and passed it over. "Good luck."

Meister dialed Ellen first. He needed to know if she was badly frightened, and to reassure her if she was. Nothing happened for a while; then an operator said, "I'm sorry, sir, but there will be no private calls for the duration of the emergency, unless you have a priority."

"Give me Emergency Code B-Nineteen, then," Meister said.

"Your group, sir?"

"Screen Team."

There was a faint sound at the outer end of the line, as if the girl had taken a quick breath. "Yes, sir," she said. "Right away." There was an angry crackle, and then the droning when the number was being rung.

"Screen Team," a voice said.

"Resonance section, please," Meister said, and when he was connected and had identified himself, a voice growled:

"Hello, Jake, this is Frank Schafer. Where the deuce are you? I sent you a telegram—but I suppose you didn't get it, the boards are jammed. Get on down here, quick!"

"No, I haven't any telegram," Meister said. "Whom do I congratulate?"

"Nobody, you fool! *We* didn't do this. We don't even know how it's been done!"

Meister felt the hairs on the back of his neck stirring. It was as if he were back in the tunnels of Concentration Camp Dora again. He swallowed and said, "But it is the antibomb screen?"

"The very thing," Schafer's tinny voice said bitterly. "Only somebody else has beat us to it—and we're trapped under it."

"It's really bombproof—you're sure of that?"

"It's anything-proof! Nothing can pass it! *And we can't get out of it, either!*"

It took quite a while to get the story straight. Project B-19, the meaningless label borne by the top-secret, billion-dollar Atomic Defense Project, was in turmoil. Much of its laboratory staff had been in the field or in Washington when the thing happened, and the jam in phone service had made it difficult to get the men who were still in the city back to the central offices.

"It's like this," Frank Schafer said, kneading a chunk of

art gum rapidly. "This dome went up last night. It lets in a little light and a few of the strongest outside radio stations nearby. But that's all—or anyhow, all that we've been able to establish so far. It's a perfect dome, over the whole island and parts of the other boroughs and New Jersey. It doesn't penetrate the ground or the water, but the only really big water frontage is way out in the harbor, so that lets out much chance of everybody swimming under it like that man from the *Miss New York.*"

"The subways are running, I heard," Meister said.

"Sure; we can evacuate the city if we have to, but not fast enough." The mobile fingers crumbled bits off the sides of the art gum. "It won't take long to breathe up the air here, and if any fires start it'll be worse. Also there's a layer of ozone about twenty feet deep all along the inside of the barrier—but don't ask me why! Even if we don't have any big blazes, we're losing oxygen at a terrific rate by ozone-fixing and surface oxidization of the ionized area."

"Ionized?" Meister frowned. "Is there much?"

"Plenty!" Schafer said. "We haven't let it out, but in another twenty hours you won't be able to hear anything on the radio but a noise like a tractor climbing a pile of cornflakes. There's been an increase already. Whatever we're using for ether these days is building up tension fast."

A runner came in from the private wires and dropped a flimsy on Frank's desk. The physicist looked at it quickly, then passed it to Meister.

"That's what I figure. You can see the spot we're in."

The message reported that oxygen was diffusing inward through the barrier at about the same rate as might be accounted for by osmosis. The figures on loss of CO_2 were less easy to establish, but it appeared that the rate here was also of an osmotic order of magnitude. It was signed by a top-notch university chemist.

"Impossible!" Meister said.

"No, it's so. And New York is entirely too big a cell to live, Jake. If we're getting oxygen only osmotically, we'll be suffocated in a week. And did you ever hear of a semipermeable membrane passing a lump of coal, or a tomato? Air, heat, food—all cut off."

"What does the Army say?"

"What they usually say: 'Do something, on the double!' We're lucky we're civilians, or we'd be court-martialed for dying!" Schafer laughed angrily and pitched the art gum away. "It's a very pretty problem, in a way," he said. "We have our antibomb screen. Now we have to find how to make ourselves *vulnerable* to the bomb—or cash in our chips. And in six days—"

The phone jangled and Schafer snatched at it. "Yeah, this is Dr. Schafer ... I'm sorry, Colonel, but we have every available man called in now except those on the Mayor's commission.... No, I don't know. Nobody knows, yet. We're tracing that radio signal now. If it has anything to do with the barrier, we'll be able to locate the generator and destroy it."

The physicist slammed the phone into its cradle and glared at Meister. "I've been taking this phone stuff all morning! I wish you'd showed up earlier. Here's the picture, briefly: The city is dying. Telephone and telegraph lines give us some communication with the outside, and we will be able to use radio inside the dome for a little while longer. There are teams outside trying to crack the barrier, but all the significant phenomena are taking place inside. Out there it just looks like a big black dome—no radiation effects, no ionization, no radio tone, no nothin'!

"We are evacuating now," he went on, "but if the dome stays up, over three quarters of the trapped people will die. If there's any fire or violence, almost all of us will die."

"You talk," Meister said, "as if you want me to kill the screen all by myself."

Schafer grinned nastily. "Sure, Jake! This barrier obviously doesn't act specifically on nuclear reactions; it stops almost everything. Almost everyone here is a nuclear man, as useless for this problem as a set of cooky-cutters. Every fact we've gotten so far shows this thing to be an immense and infinitely complicated form of cavity-resonance—and you're the only resonance engineer inside."

The grin disappeared. Schafer said, "We can give you all the electronics technicians you need, plenty of official backing, and general theoretical help. It's not much but it's all we've got. We estimate about eleven million people inside this box—eleven million corpses unless you can get the lid off it."

Meister nodded. Somehow, the problem did not weigh as heavily upon him as it might have. He was remembering Dora, the wasted bodies jammed under the stairs, in storerooms, fed into the bake-oven five at a time. One could survive almost anything if one had had practice in surviving. There was only Ellen—

Ellen was probably in The Box—the dome. That meant something, while eleven million was only a number.

"Entdecken," he murmured.

Schafer looked up at him, his blue eyes snapping sparks. Schafer certainly didn't look like one of the world's best nuclear physicists. Schafer was a sandy-haired runt—with the bomb hung over his head by a horsehair.

"What's that?" he said.

"A German word," Meister answered. "It means, to discover—literally, to take the roof off. That is the first step, it seems. To take the roof off, we must discover that transmitter."

"I've got men out with loop antennas. The geometrical center of the dome is right at the tip of the Empire State

Building, but WNBT says there's nothing up there but their television transmitters."

"What they mean," Meister said, "is that there was nothing else up there two weeks ago. There *must* be a radiator at a radiant point no matter how well it is disguised."

"I'll send a team." Schafer got up, fumbling for the art gum he had thrown away. "I'll go myself, I guess. I'm jittery here."

"With your teeth? I would not advise it. You would die slain, as the Italians say!"

"Teeth?" Schafer said. He giggled nervously. "What's that got to—"

"You have metal in your mouth. If the mast is actually radiating this effect, your jawbones might be burned out of your head. Get a group with perfect teeth, or porcelain fillings at best. And wear nothing with metal in it, not even shoes."

"Oh," Schafer said. "I knew we needed you, Jake." He rubbed the back of his hand over his forehead and reached into his shirt pocket for a cigarette.

Meister struck it out of his hand. "Six days' oxygen remaining," he said.

Schafer lunged up out of his chair, aimed a punch at Meister's head, and fainted across the desk.

The dim city stank of ozone. The street lights were still on. Despite radioed warnings to stay indoors, surging mobs struggled senselessly toward the barrier. Counter-waves surged back, coughing, from the unbreathable stuff pouring out from it. More piled up in subway stations; people screamed and trampled one another. Curiously, the city's take that day was enormous. Not even disaster could break the deeply entrenched habit of putting a token in the turnstile.

The New York Central and Long Island Railroads,

whose tracks were above ground, where the screen cut across them, were shut down, as were the underground lines which came to the surface inside The Box. Special trains were running every three minutes from Pennsylvania Station, with passengers jamming the aisles and platforms.

In the Hudson Tubes the situation was worse. So great was the crush of fleeing humans there, they could hardly operate at all. The screen drew a lethal line between Hoboken and Newark, so that Tube trains had to make the longer of the two trips to get their passengers out of The Box. A brief power interruption stopped one train in complete darkness for ten minutes beneath the Hudson River, and terror and madness swept through it.

Queens and Brooklyn subways siphoned off a little pressure, but only a little. In a major disaster the normal human impulse is to go north, on the map-fostered myth that north is "up."

Navy launches were readied to ferry as many as cared to make the try out to where The Box lay over the harbor and the rivers, but thus far there were no such swimmers. Very few people can swim twenty feet under water, and to come up for air short of that twenty feet would be disastrous. That would be as fatal as coming up in the barrier itself; ozone is lung-rot in high concentrations. That alone kept most of the foolhardy from trying to run through the wall—that, and the gas-masked police cordon.

From Governor's Island, about half of which was in The Box, little Army ferries shipped over several cases of small arms which were distributed to subway and railroad guards. Two detachments of infantry also came along, relieving a little of the strain on the police.

Meister, hovering with two technicians and the helicopter pilot over a building on the edge of the screen, peered downward in puzzlement. It was hard to make any sense of the geometry of shadows below him.

"Give me the phone," he said.

The senior technician passed him the mike. A comparatively long-wave channel had been cleared by a major station for the use of emergency teams and prowl cars, since nothing could be heard on short-wave above that eternal humming.

"Frank, are you on?" Meister called. "Any word from Ellen yet?"

"No, but her landlady says she went to Jersey to visit yesterday," came over the air waves. There was an unspoken understanding between them that the hysterical attack of an hour ago would not be mentioned. "You'll have to crack The Box to get more news, I guess, Jake. See anything yet?"

"Nothing but more trouble. Have you thought yet about heat conservation? I am reminded that it is summer; we will soon have an oven here."

"I thought of that, but it isn't so," Frank Schafer's voice said. "It seems hotter only because there's no wind. Actually, the Weather Bureau says we're *losing* heat pretty rapidly; they expect the drop to level at fifteen to twenty above."

Meister whistled. "So low! Yet there is a steady supply of calories in the water—"

"Water's a poor conductor. What worries me is this accursed ozone. It's diffusing through the city—already smells like the inside of a transformer around here!"

"What about the Empire State Building?"

"Not a thing. We ran soap bubbles along the power leads to see if something was tapping some of WNBT's power, but there isn't a break in them anywhere. Maybe you'd better go over there when you're through at the barrier. There are some things we can't make sense of."

"I shall," Meister said. "I will leave here as soon as I start a fire."

Schafer began to sputter. Meister smiled gently and handed the phone back to the technician.

"Break out the masks," he said. "We can go down now."

A rooftop beside the barrier was like some hell dreamed up in the violent ward of a hospital. Every movement accumulated a small static charge on the surface of the body, which discharged stingingly and repeatedly from the fingertips and even the tip of the nose if it approached a grounded object too closely.

Only a few yards away was the unguessable wall itself, smooth, deep gray, featureless, yet somehow quivering with a pseudo-life of its own—a shimmering haze just too dense to penetrate. It had no definite boundary. Instead, the tarpaper over which it lay here began to dim, and within a foot faded into the general mystery.

Meister looked at the barrier. The absence of anything upon which the eye could fasten was dizzying. The mind made up patterns and flashes of lurid color and projected them into the grayness. Sometimes it seemed that the fog extended for miles. A masked policeman stepped over from the inside parapet and touched him on the elbow.

"Wouldn't look at her too long, sir," he said. "We've had ambulances below carting away sightseers who forgot to look away. Pretty soon your eyes sort of get fixed."

Meister nodded. The thing was hypnotic all right. And yet the eye was drawn to it because it was the only source of light here. The ionization was so intense that it bled off power from the lines, so that street lamps had gone off all around the edge. From the helicopter, the city had looked as if its rim were inked out in a vast ring. Meister could feel the individual hairs all over his body stirring; it made him feel infested. Well, there'd been no shortage of lice at Dora!

Behind him the technicians were unloading the apparatus from the 'copter. Meister beckoned. "Get a reading on field strength first of all," he said gloomily. "Whoever is doing this has plenty of power. Ionized gas, a difficult achievement—"

He stopped suddenly. Not so difficult. The city was enclosed; it was, in effect, a giant Geissler tube. Of course the concentration of rare gases was not high enough to produce a visible glow, but—

"Plenty high," the technician with the loop said. "Between forty-five and fifty thousand. Seems to be rising a little, too."

"Between—" Meister stepped quickly to the instrument. Sure enough, the black needle was wavering, so rapidly as to be only a fan-shaped blur between the two figures. "This is ridiculous! Is that instrument reliable?"

"I just took the underwriters' seal off it," the technician said. "Did you figure this much ozone could be fixed out without any alteration?"

"Yes, I had presupposed the equivalent of UV bombardment. This changes things. No wonder there is light leaking through that screen! Sergeant—"

"Yes sir?" the policeman mumbled through his mask.

"How much of the area below can you clear?"

"As much as you need."

"Good." Meister reached into his jacket pocket and produced the map of the city the pilot had given him. "We are here, yes? Make a cordon, then, from here to here." His soft pencil scrawled a black line around four buildings. "Then get as much fire-fighting equipment outside the line as you can muster."

"You're expecting a bad fire?"

"No, a *good* one. But hurry!"

The cop scratched his head in puzzlement, but he went below. Meister smiled. Members of the Screen Team were the Mister Bigs in this city now. Twenty hours ago nobody'd ever heard of the Screen Team.

The technician, working with nervous quickness, was tying an oscilloscope into the loop circuit. Meister nodded approvingly. If there was a pulse to this phenomenon, it would be just as well to know its form. He snapped his fingers.

"What's wrong, Doctor?"

"My memory. I have put my head on backwards when I got up this morning, I think. We will have to photograph the waveform; it will be too complex to analyze here."

"How do you know?" the technician asked.

"By that radio tone," Meister said. "You Americans work by sight. There are almost no resonance electronics men in this country. But in Germany we worked as much by ear as by eye. Where you convert a wave into a visible pattern, we turned it into an audible one. We had a saying that resonance engineers were disappointed musicians."

The face of the tube suddenly produced a green wiggle. It was the kind of wiggle a crazy man might make. The technician looked at it in dismay. "That," he said, "doesn't exist. I won't work in a science where it *could* exist!"

Meister grinned. "That is what I meant. The radio sound was a fundamental B-flat, but with hundreds of harmonics and overtones. You don't have it all in the field yet."

"I don't?" He looked. "So I don't! But when I reduce it that much, you can't see the shape of the modulations."

"We will have to photograph it by sections."

Bringing over the camera, the other man set it up. They worked rapidly, oppressed by the unnatural pearly glimmer, the masks, the stink of ozone which crept in at the sides of the treated cloth, the electrical prickling, above all by the silent terror of any trapped animal.

While they worked, the cop came back and stood by silently, watching. The gas mask gave no indication of his expression, but Meister could feel the pressure of faith radiating from the man. Doubtless these bits of equipment were meaningless to him—but bits of equipment like these had put up The Box, beyond the powers of policemen or presidents to take it down again. Men who knew about such things were as good as gods now.

Unless they failed.

"That does it," the technician said.

The cop stepped forward. "I've got the area you marked roped off," he said diffidently. "We've searched the apartments and there's nobody in them. If there's any fire here, we'll be able to control it."

"Excellent!" Meister said. "Remember that this gas will feed the flames, however. You will need every possible man."

"Yes sir. Anything else?"

"Just get out of the district yourself."

Meister climbed into the plane and stood by the open hatch, looking at his wrist watch. He gave the cop ten minutes to leave the tenement and get out to the fire lines. Then he struck a match and pitched it out onto the roof.

"Up!" he shouted.

The rotors roared. The pitch on the roof began to smolder. A tongue of flame shot up. In three seconds the whole side of the roof nearest the gray screen was blazing.

The helicopter lurched and clawed for altitude.

Behind the plane arose a brilliant and terrifying yellow glare. Meister didn't bother to watch it. He squatted with his back to the fire and waved pieces of paper over the neck of a bottle.

The ammonia fumes were invisible and couldn't be smelled through the mask, but on the dry-plates wiggly lines were appearing. Meister studied them, nibbling gently at his lower lip. With luck, the lines would answer one question at least: they would tell what The Box was. With luck, they might even tell how it was produced.

They would *not* tell where it came from.

The motion of the 'copter changed suddenly, and Meister's stomach stirred uneasily under his belt. He stowed the plates and looked up. The foreshortened spire of the Empire State Building pointed up at him through the transparent deck; another 'copter hovered at its tip. The television antennas were hidden now in what seemed to be a globe of some dark substance.

Meister picked up the radio-phone. "Schafer?" he called—this to the Empire State Building.

"No, this is Talliafero," came back an answer. "Schafer's back at the labs. We're about ready to leave. Need any help?"

"I don't think so," Meister said. "Is that foil you have around the tower mast?"

"Yes, but it's only a precaution. The whole tower's radiating. The foil radiates, too, now that we've got it up. See you later."

The other 'copter stirred and swooped away.

Meister twisted the dial up into the short-wave region. The humming surged in; he valved down the volume and listened intently. The sound was different somehow. After a moment his mind placed it. The fundamental B-flat was still there, but some of the overtones were gone; that meant that hundreds of them, which the little amplifier could not reproduce, were also gone. He was listening on an FM set; his little table set at the apartment was AM. So the wave was modulated along both axes, and probably pulse-modulated as well. But why should it simplify as one approached its source?

Resonance, of course. The upper harmonics were echoes. Yet a simple primary tone in a well-known frequency range couldn't produce The Box by itself. It was the harmonics that made the difference, and the harmonics couldn't appear without the existence of some chamber like The Box. Along this line of reasoning, The Box was a precondition of its own existence. Meister felt his head swimming.

"Hey," the pilot said. "It's started to snow!"

Meister turned off the set and looked out. "All right, let's go home now."

Despite its depleted staff, the Screen Team was quiet with the intense hush of concentration that was its equivalent of roaring activity. Frank Schafer's door was closed, but Meister didn't bother to knock. He was on the edge of an idea and there was no time to be lost in formalities.

There were a number of uniformed men in the office with Frank. There was also a big man in expensive clothes, and a smaller man who looked as if he needed sleep. The smaller man had dark circles under his eyes, but despite his haggardness Meister knew him. The mayor. The big man did not look familiar—nor pleasant.

As for the high brass, nothing in a uniform looked pleasant to Meister. He pushed forward and put the dry-plates down on Schafer's desk. "The resonance products," he said. "If we can duplicate the fundamental in the lab—"

There came a roar from the big man. "Dr. Schafer, is this the man we've been waiting for?"

Schafer made a tired gesture. "Jake, this is Roland Dean," he said. "You know the mayor, I think. These others are security officers. They seem to think you made The Box."

Meister stiffened. "I? That's idiotic!"

"Any noncitizen is automatically under suspicion," one of the Army men said. "However, Dr. Schafer exaggerates. We just want to ask a few questions."

The mayor coughed. He was obviously tired, and the taint of ozone did not make breathing very comfortable.

"I'm afraid there's more to it than that, Dr. Meister," he

added. "Mr. Dean here has insisted upon an arrest. I'd like to say for myself that I think it all quite stupid."

"Thank you," Meister said. "What is Mr. Dean's interest in this?"

"Mr. Dean," Schafer growled, "is the owner of that block of tenements you're burning out up north. The fire's spreading, by the way. When I told him I didn't know why you lit it, he blew his top."

"Why not?" Dean said, glaring at Meister. "I fail to see why this emergency should be made an excuse for irresponsible destruction of property. Have you any reason for burning my buildings, Meister?"

"Are you having any trouble with breathing, Mr. Dean?" Meister asked.

"Certainly! Who isn't? Do you think you can make it easier for us by filling The Box with smoke?"

Meister nodded. "I gather that you have no knowledge of elementary chemistry, Mr. Dean. The Box is rapidly converting our oxygen into an unbreathable form. A good hot fire will consume some of it, but it will also break up the ozone molecules. The ratio is about two atoms of oxygen consumed for every one set free—out of three which in the form of ozone could not have been breathed at all."

Schafer sighed gustily. "I should have guessed. A neat scheme, Jake. But what about the ratio between reduction of ozone and over-all oxygen consumption?"

"Large enough to maintain five of the six days' grace with which we started. Had we let the ozone-fixing process continue unabated, we should not have lasted forty hours longer."

"Mumbo jumbo!" Dean said stonily, turning to Schafer. "A halfway measure. The problem is to get us out of this mess, not to stretch our sufferings out by three days by invading property rights. This man is a German, probably a Nazi! By your own admission, he's the only man in your whole section who's seemed to know what to do. And nothing he's done so far has shown any result, except to destroy some of my buildings!"

"Dr. Meister, just what *has* been accomplished thus far?" a colonel of Intelligence said.

"Only a few tentative observations," Meister said. "We have most of the secondary phenomena charted."

"Charts!" Dean snorted.

"Can you offer any assurance that The Box will be down in time?" the colonel asked.

"That," Meister said, "would be very foolish of me. The possibility exists, that is all. Certainly it will take time—we have barely scratched the surface."

"In that case, I'm afraid you'll have to consider yourself under arrest—"

"See here, Colonel!" Schafer surged to his feet, his face flushed. "Don't you know that he's the only man in The Box who can crack it? That fire was good common sense. If you arrest my men for *not* doing anything, we'll never get anything done!"

"I am not exactly stupid, Dr. Schafer," the colonel said harshly. "I have no interest in Mr. Dean's tenements, and if the mayor is forced to jail Dr. Meister we will spring him at once. All I'm interested in is the chance that Dr. Meister may be *maintaining* The Box instead of trying to *crack it.*"

"Explain, please," Meister said mildly.

Pulling himself up to military straightness, the colonel cleared his throat and said:

"You're inside The Box. If you put it up, you have a way out of it, and know where the generator is. You may go where you please, but from now on we'll have a guard with you. . . . Satisfied, Dr. Schafer?"

"It doesn't satisfy me!" Dean rumbled. "What about my property? Are you going to let this madman burn buildings with a guard to help?"

The colonel looked at the landlord. "Mr. Dean," he said quietly, "you seem to think The Box was created to annoy you personally. The Army hasn't the technical knowledge to destroy it, but it has sense enough to realize that more than just New York is under attack here. The enemy, whoever he may be, thinks his screen uncrackable, otherwise he wouldn't have given us this chance to work on it by boxing in one city alone. If The Box is not down in, say, eight days, he'll know that New York failed and died—and every city in the country will be bombed to slag the next morning."

Schafer sat down again, looking surly. "Why?" he asked the army man. "Why would they waste the bombs when they could just box in the cities?"

"Inefficient. America's too big to occupy except slowly, piecemeal. They'd have no reason to care if large parts of it were uninhabitable for a while. The important thing is to knock us out as a military force, as a power in world affairs."

"If they boxed in all the cities at once—"

The colonel shook his head. "We have rocket emplacements of our own, and they *aren't* in large cities. Neither Box nor bomb would catch more than a few of them. No. They have to know that The Box is uncrackable, so they can screen their own cities against our bombs until our whole country is knocked out. With The Box, that would take more than a week, and their cities would suffer along with ours. With bombs, a day would be enough. So they've allowed us this test. If New York comes out of this, there'll be no attack, at least until they've gotten a better screen. The Box seems good enough so far!"

"Politics," Schafer said, shaking his head disgustedly. "It's much too devious for me! Doesn't The Box constitute an attack?"

"Certainly—but who's doing the attacking?" the colonel

demanded. "We can guess, but we don't know. And I doubt very much that the enemy has left any traces."

Meister stiffened suddenly, a thrill of astonishment shooting up his backbone. Schafer stared at him.

"Traces!" Meister said. "Of course! That is what has been stopping us all along. Naturally there would be no traces. We have been wasting time looking for them. Frank, the generator is not in the Empire State Building. *It is not even in The Box!*"

"But, Jake, it's got to be," Schafer said. "It's physically impossible for it to be outside!"

"A trick," Dean rumbled.

Meister waved his hands excitedly. "No, no! This is the reasoning which has made our work so fruitless. Observe. As the colonel says, the enemy would not dare leave traces. Now, workmanship is traceable, particularly if the device is revolutionary, as this one is. Find that generator and you know at once which country has made it. You observe the principle, and you say to yourself, 'Ah, yes, there were reports, rumors, whispers of shadows of rumors of such a principle, but I discounted them as fantasy; they came out of Country X.' Do you follow?"

"Yes, but—"

"But no country would leave such a fingerprint where it could be found. This we can count upon. Whereas we know as yet next to nothing about the physics of The Box. Therefore, if it is physically impossible for the generator to be outside The Box, this does not mean that we must continue to search for it inside. It means that we must find a physical principle which makes it possible to be outside!"

Frank Schafer threw up his hands. "Revise basic physics in a week! Well, let's try. I suppose Meister's allowed lab work, Colonel?"

"Certainly, as long as my guards aren't barred from the laboratory."

Thirty hours later the snow stopped falling, leaving a layer a little over three inches deep. The battling mobs were no longer on the streets. Hopeless masses were jammed body to body in railroad stations and subways. The advancing ozone had driven the people in upon themselves, and into the houses and basements where rooms could be sealed against the searing stench.

Thousands had already died along the periphery. The New Jersey and Brooklyn shores were charnel heaps of those who had fought to get back across the river to Manhattan and cleaner air. The tenements along the West Side of the island still blazed—twenty linear blocks of them—but the fire had failed to jump Ninth Avenue and was dying for want of fuel. Elsewhere it was very cold. The city was dying.

Over it, The Box was invisible. It was the third night.

In the big lab at the Team office, Meister, Schafer, and the two technicians suddenly disappeared under a little Box of their own, leaving behind four frantic soldiers. Meister sighed gustily and looked at the black screen a few feet from his head.

"Now we know," he said. "Frank, you can turn on the light now."

The desk lamp clicked on. In the shaded glow Meister saw that tears were trickling down Schafer's cheeks.

"No, no, don't weep yet, the job is not quite done!" Meister cried. "But see—so simple, so beautiful!" He gestured at the lump of metal in the exact center of the Boxed area. "Here we are—four men, a bit of metallic trash, an empty desk, a lamp, a cup of foil. Where is the screen generator? Outside!"

Schafer swallowed. "But it isn't," he said hoarsely. "Oh, you were right, Jake—the key projector *is* outside. But it doesn't generate the screen; it just excites the iron there, and that does the job." He looked at the scattered graphs on the desk top. "I'd never have dreamed such a jam of fields were possible! Look at those waves—catching each other, heterodyning, slowing each other up as the tension increases. No wonder the whole structure of space gives way when they finally get in phase!"

One of the technicians looked nervously at the little Box and cleared his throat. "I still don't see why it should leak light, oxygen, and so forth, even the little that it does. The jam has to be radiated away, and the screen should be the subspatial equivalent of a perfect radiator, a black body. But it's gray."

"No, it's black," Schafer said. "But it isn't turned on all the time. If it were, the catalyst radiation couldn't get through. It's a perfect electromagnetic push-me-pull-you. The apparatus outside projects the catalyst fields in. The lump of iron—in this case the Empire State Building—is excited and throws off the screen fields. The screen goes up. The screen cuts off the catalyst radiation. The screen goes down. In comes the primary beam again. And so on. The kicker is that without the off-again-on-again, you wouldn't get anything—the screen couldn't exist because the intermittence supplies some of the necessary harmonics."

He grinned ruefully. "Here I am explaining it as if I understood it. You're a good teacher, Jake!"

"Once one realizes that the screen has to *be* up before it can *go* up," Meister said, grinning back, "one has the rest—or most of it. Introducing a rhythmic interruption of the very first pulses is a simple trick. The hardest thing about it is timing—to know just when the screen goes up for the first time, so that the blinker can be cut out at precisely that moment."

"So how do we get out?"

"Feedback," Meister said. "There must be an enormous back EMF in the incoming beam. And whether it is converted and put back into the system again at the source, or just efficiently wasted, we can burn it out." He consulted a chalk line which ran along the floor from the edge of the little Box to the lump of iron, then picked up the cup of foil and pointed it along the mark away from the lump. "The trick," he said soberly, "is not to nullify, but to amplify—"

The glare of the overheads burst in upon them. The lab was jammed with soldiers, all with rifles at the ready and all the rifles pointing in at them. The smell of burned insulation curled from an apparatus at the other end of the chalk line.

"Oh," said Schafer. "We forgot the most important thing! Which way does our chalk line run from the Empire State Building, I wonder?"

"It could be anywhere above the horizon," Meister said. "Try pointing your reflector straight up, first."

Schafer swore. "Anytime you want a diploma for unscrewing the inscrutable, Jake," he said, "I'll write you one with my nose!"

It was cold and quiet now in the city. The fires on the West Side, where one of the country's worst slums had been burned out, smoldered and flickered.

The air was a slow, cumulative poison. It was very dark.

On top of the Empire State Building a great, shining bowl swung in a certain direction, stopped, waited. Fifty miles above it, in a region where neither *cold* nor *air* have any human meaning, a clumsy torpedo began to warm slightly. Inside it, delicate things glowed, fused—melted. There was no other difference; the torpedo kept on, traveled at its assigned twenty-one and eight-tenths miles per minute. It would always do so.

The Box vanished. The morning sunlight glared in. There was a torrent of rain as cold air hit hot July. Within minutes the city was as gray as before, but with roiling thunderheads. People poured out of the buildings into the downpour, hysterical faces turned to the free air, shouting amid the thunder, embracing each other, dancing in the lightning flares.

The storm passed almost at once, but the dancing went on quite a while.

"Traces!" Meister said to Frank Schafer. "Where else could you hide them? An orbital missile was the only answer."

"That sunlight," Schafer said, "sure looks good! You'd better go home to bed, Jake, before the official hero worshipers catch up with you."

But Meister was already dreamlessly asleep.

The Dead Past

ISAAC ASIMOV

Surely a device that would allow historians to peer at the events of past centuries holds great value for mankind. To be able to trace historical cause and effect with total accuracy, to look upon the actual faces of antiquity's greatest leaders, to correct the errors that accumulate through many retellings of the same story—what a marvelous boon!
But, as Isaac Asimov shows us here, even the most beneficial of inventions may have its hidden drawbacks, its unexpected troublesome consequences.

ARNOLD POTTERLEY, Ph.D., was a Professor of Ancient History. That, in itself, was not dangerous. What changed the world beyond all dreams was the fact that he *looked* like a Professor of Ancient History.

Thaddeus Araman, Department Head of the Division of Chronoscopy, might have taken proper action if Dr. Potterley had been owner of a large, square chin, flashing eyes, aquiline nose and broad shoulders.

As it was, Thaddeus Araman found himself staring over his desk at a mild-mannered individual, whose faded blue eyes looked at him wistfully from either side of a low-bridged button nose; whose small, neatly dressed figure seemed stamped "milk-and-water" from thinning brown hair to the neatly brushed shoes that completed a conservative middle-class costume.

Araman said pleasantly, "And now what can I do for you, Dr. Potterley?"

Dr. Potterley said in a soft voice that went well with the

rest of him, "Mr. Araman, I came to you because you're top man in chronoscopy."

Araman smiled. "Not exactly. Above me is the World Commissioner of Research and above him is the Secretary-General of the United Nations. And above both of them, of course, are the sovereign peoples of Earth."

Dr. Potterley shook his head. "They're not interested in chronoscopy. I've come to you, sir, because for two years I have been trying to obtain permission to do some time viewing—chronoscopy, that is—in connection with my researches on ancient Carthage. I can't obtain such permission. My research grants are all proper. There is no irregularity in any of my intellectual endeavors and yet—"

"I'm sure there is no question of irregularity," said Araman soothingly. He flipped the thin reproduction sheets in the folder to which Potterley's name had been attached. They had been produced by Multivac, whose vast analogical mind kept all the department records. When this was over, the sheets could be destroyed, then reproduced on demand in a matter of minutes.

And while Araman turned the pages, Dr. Potterley's voice continued in a soft monotone.

The historian was saying, "I must explain that my problem is quite an important one. Carthage was ancient commercialism brought to its zenith. Pre-Roman Carthage was the nearest ancient analogue to pre-atomic America, at least insofar as its attachment to trade, commerce and business in general was concerned. They were the most daring seamen and explorers before the Vikings; much better at it than the overrated Greeks.

"To know Carthage would be very rewarding, yet the only knowledge we have of it is derived from the writings of its bitter enemies, the Greeks and Romans. Carthage itself never wrote in its own defense or, if it did, the books did not survive. As a result, the Carthaginians have been one of the favorite sets of villains of history and perhaps unjustly so. Time viewing may set the record straight."

He said much more.

Araman said, still turning the reproduction sheets before him, "You must realize, Dr. Potterley, that chronoscopy, or time viewing, if you prefer, is a difficult process."

Dr. Potterley, who had been interrupted, frowned and said, "I am asking for only certain selected views at times and places I would indicate."

Araman sighed. "Even a few views, even one ... It is an unbelievably delicate art. There is the question of focus, getting the proper scene in view and holding it. There is the synchronization of sound, which calls for completely independent circuits."

"Surely my problem is important enough to justify considerable effort."

"Yes, sir. Undoubtedly," said Araman at once. To deny the importance of someone's research problem would be unforgivably bad manners. "But you must understand how long drawn out even the simplest view is. And there is a long waiting line for the chronoscope and an even longer waiting line for the use of Multivac which guides us in our use of the controls."

Potterley stirred unhappily. "But can nothing be done? For two years—"

"A matter of priority, sir. I'm sorry. . . . Cigarette?"

The historian started back at the suggestion, eyes suddenly widening as he stared at the pack thrust out toward him. Araman looked surprised, withdrew the pack, made a motion as though to take a cigarette for himself and thought better of it.

Potterley drew a sigh of unfeigned relief as the pack was put out of sight. He said, "Is there any way of reviewing matters, putting me as far forward as possible? I don't know how to explain—"

Araman smiled. Some had offered money under similar

circumstances which, of course, had gotten them nowhere, either. He said, "The decisions on priority are
computer-processed. I could in no way alter those decisions arbitrarily."

Potterley rose stiffly to his feet. He stood five and a half
feet tall. "Then, good day, sir."

"Good day, Dr. Potterley. And my sincerest regrets."

He offered his hand and Potterley touched it briefly.

The historian left, and a touch of the buzzer brought
Araman's secretary into the room. He handed her the
folder.

"These," he said, "may be disposed of."

Alone again, he smiled bitterly. Another item in his
quarter-century service to the human race. Service
through negation.

At least this fellow had been easy to dispose of. Sometimes academic pressure had to be applied and even
withdrawal of grants.

Five minutes later, he had forgotten Dr. Potterley. Nor,
thinking back on it later, could he remember feeling any
premonition of danger.

During the first year of his frustration, Arnold Potterley
had experienced only that—frustration. During the second year, though, his frustration gave birth to an idea
that first frightened and then fascinated him. Two things
stopped him from trying to translate the idea into action,
and neither barrier was the undoubted fact that his notion
was a grossly unethical one.

The first was merely the continuing hope that the government would finally give its permission and make it
unnecessary for him to do anything more. That hope had
perished finally in the interview with Araman just completed.

The second barrier had been not a hope at all but a
dreary realization of his own incapacity. He was not a
physicist and he knew no physicists from whom he might

obtain help. The Department of Physics at the university consisted of men well stocked with grants and well immersed in specialty. At best, they would not listen to him. At worst, they would report him for intellectual anarchy and even his basic Carthaginian grant might easily be withdrawn.

That he could not risk. And yet chronoscopy was the only way to carry on his work. Without it, he would be no worse off if his grant were lost.

The first hint that the second barrier might be overcome had come a week earlier than his interview with Araman, and it had gone unrecognized at the time. It had been at one of the faculty teas. Potterley attended these sessions unfailingly because he conceived attendance to be a duty, and he took his duties seriously. Once there, however, he conceived it to be no responsibility of his to make light conversation or new friends. He sipped abstemiously at a drink or two, exchanged a polite word with the dean or such department heads as happened to be present, bestowed a narrow smile on others and finally left early.

Ordinarily, he would have paid no attention, at that most recent tea, to a young man standing quietly, even diffidently, in one corner. He would never have dreamed of speaking to him. Yet a tangle of circumstance persuaded him this once to behave in a way contrary to his nature.

That morning at breakfast, Mrs. Potterley had announced somberly that once again she had dreamed of Laurel; but this time a Laurel grown up, yet retaining the three-year-old face that stamped her as their child. Potterley had let her talk. There had been a time when he fought her too frequent preoccupation with the past and death. Laurel would not come back to them, either through dreams or through talk. Yet if it appeased Caroline Potterley—let her dream and talk.

But when Potterley went to school that morning, he found himself for once affected by Caroline's inanities. Laurel grown up! She had died nearly twenty years ago; their only child, then and ever. In all that time, when he thought of her, it was as a three-year-old.

Now he thought: But if she were alive now, she wouldn't be three, she'd be nearly twenty-three.

Helplessly, he found himself trying to think of Laurel as growing progressively older; as finally becoming twenty-three. He did not quite succeed.

Yet he tried. Laurel using make-up. Laurel going out with boys. Laurel—getting married!

So it was that when he saw the young man hovering at the outskirts of the coldly circulating group of faculty men, it occurred to him quixotically that, for all he knew, a youngster just such as this might have married Laurel. That youngster himself, perhaps . . .

Laurel might have met him, here at the university, or some evening when he might be invited to dinner at the Potterleys'. They might grow interested in one another. Laurel would surely have been pretty and this youngster looked well. He was dark in coloring, with a lean, intent face and an easy carriage.

The tenuous daydream snapped, yet Potterley found himself staring foolishly at the young man, not as a strange face but as a possible son-in-law in the might-have-been. He found himself threading his way toward the man. It was almost a form of autohypnotism.

He put out his hand. "I am Arnold Potterley of the History Department. You're new here, I think?"

The youngster looked faintly astonished and fumbled with his drink, shifting it to his left hand in order to shake with his right. "Jonas Foster is my name, sir. I'm a new instructor in physics. I'm just starting this semester."

Potterley nodded. "I wish you a happy stay here and great success."

That was the end of it, then. Potterley had come uneasily to his senses, found himself embarrassed and moved off. He stared back over his shoulder once, but the illusion of relationship had gone. Reality was quite real once more and he was angry with himself for having fallen prey to his wife's foolish talk about Laurel.

But a week later, even while Araman was talking, the thought of that young man had come back to him. An instructor in physics. A new instructor. Had he been deaf at the time? Was there a short circuit between ear and brain? Or was it an automatic self-censorship because of the impending interview with the Head of Chronoscopy?

But the interview failed, and it was the thought of the young man with whom he had exchanged two sentences that prevented Potterley from elaborating his pleas for consideration. He was almost anxious to get away.

And in the autogiro express back to the university, he could almost wish he were superstitious. He could then console himself with the thought that the casual meaningless meeting had really been directed by a knowing and purposeful Fate.

Jonas Foster was not new to academic life. The long and rickety struggle for the doctorate would make anyone a veteran. Additional work as a postdoctorate teaching fellow acted as a booster shot.

But now he was Instructor Jonas Foster. Professorial dignity lay ahead. And he now found himself in a new sort of relationship toward other professors.

For one thing, they would be voting on future promotions. For another, he was in no position to tell so early in the game which particular member of the faculty might or might not have the ear of the dean or even of the university president. He did not fancy himself as a campus politician and was sure he would make a poor one, yet there was no point in kicking his own rear into blisters just to prove that to himself.

So Foster listened to this mild-mannered historian who, in some vague way, seemed nevertheless to radiate tension, and did not shut him up abruptly and toss him out. Certainly that was his first impulse.

He remembered Potterley well enough. Potterley had approached him at that tea (which had been a grizzly affair). The fellow had spoken two sentences to him stiffly, somehow glassy-eyed, had then come to himself with a visible start and hurried off.

It had amused Foster at the time, but now . . .

Potterley might have been deliberately trying to make his acquaintance, or, rather, to impress his own personality on Foster as that of a queer sort of duck, eccentric but harmless. He might now be probing Foster's views, searching for unsettling opinions. Surely, they ought to have done so before granting him his appointment. Still . . .

Potterley might be serious, might honestly not realize what he was doing. Or he might realize quite well what he was doing; he might be nothing more or less than a dangerous rascal.

Foster mumbled, "Well, now—" to gain time, and fished out a package of cigarettes, intending to offer one to Potterley and to light it and one for himself very slowly.

But Potterley said at once, "Please, Dr. Foster. No cigarettes."

Foster looked startled. "I'm sorry, sir."

"No. The regrets are mine. I cannot stand the odor. An idiosyncrasy. I'm sorry."

He was positively pale. Foster put away the cigarettes.

Foster, feeling the absence of the cigarette, took the easy way out. "I'm flattered that you ask my advice and all that, Dr. Potterley, but I'm not a neutrinics man. I can't very well do anything professional in that direction. Even stating an opinion would be out of line, and, frankly, I'd prefer that you didn't go into any particulars."

The historian's prim face set hard. "What do you mean, you're not a neutrinics man? You're not anything yet. You haven't received any grant, have you?"

"This is only my first semester."

"I know that. I imagine you haven't even applied for any grant yet."

Foster half smiled. In three months at the university, he had not succeeded in putting his initial requests for research grants into good enough shape to pass on to a professional science writer, let alone to the Research Commission.

(His Department Head, fortunately, took it quite well. "Take your time now, Foster," he said, "and get your thoughts well organized. Make sure you know your path and where it will lead, for, once you receive a grant, your specialization will be formally recognized and, for better or for worse, it will be yours for the rest of your career." The advice was trite enough, but triteness has often the merit of truth, and Foster recognized that.)

Foster said, "By education and inclination, Dr. Potterley, I'm a hyperoptics man with a gravitics minor. It's how I described myself in applying for this position. It may not be my official specialization yet, but it's going to be. It can't be anything else. As for neutrinics, I never even studied the subject."

"Why not?" demanded Potterley at once.

Foster stared. It was the kind of rude curiosity about another man's professional status that was always irritating. He said, with the edge of his own politeness just a trifle blunted, "A course in neutrinics wasn't given at my university."

"Good Lord, where did you go?"

"M.I.T.," said Foster quietly.

"And they don't teach neutrinics?"

"No, they don't." Foster felt himself flush and was moved to a defense. "It's a highly specialized subject with no great value. Chronoscopy, perhaps, has some value, but it is the only practical application and that's a dead end."

The historian stared at him earnestly. "Tell me this. Do you know where I can find a neutrinics man?"

"No, I don't," said Foster bluntly.

"Well, then, do you know a school which teaches neutrinics?"

"No, I don't."

Potterley smiled tightly and without humor.

Foster resented that smile, found he detected insult in it and grew sufficiently annoyed to say, "I would like to point out, sir, that you're stepping out of line."

"What?"

"I'm saying that, as a historian, your interest in any sort of physics, your *professional* interest, is—" He paused, unable to bring himself quite to say the word.

"Unethical?"

"That's the word, Dr. Potterley."

"My researches have driven me to it," said Potterley in an intense whisper.

"The Research Commission is the place to go. If they permit—"

"I have gone to them and have received no satisfaction."

"Then obviously you must abandon this." Foster knew he was sounding stuffily virtuous, but he wasn't going to let this man lure him into an expression of intellectual anarchy. It was too early in his career to take stupid risks.

Apparently, though, the remark had its effect on Potterley. Without any warning, the man exploded into a rapid-fire verbal storm of irresponsibility.

Scholars, he said, could be free only if they could freely follow their own free-swinging curiosity. Research, he said, forced into a predesigned pattern by the powers that held the purse strings became slavish and had to stagnate. No man, he said, had the right to dictate the intellectual interests of another.

Foster listened to all of it with disbelief. None of it was strange to him. He had heard college boys talk so in order to shock their professors and he had once or twice amused himself in that fashion, too. Anyone who studied the history of science knew that many men had once thought so.

Yet it seemed strange to Foster, almost against nature, that a modern man of science could advance such nonsense. No one would advocate running a factory by allowing each individual worker to do whatever pleased him at the moment, or of running a ship according to the casual and conflicting notions of each individual crewman. It would be taken for granted that some sort of centralized supervisory agency must exist in each case. Why should direction and order benefit a factory and a ship but not scientific research?

People might say that the human mind was somehow qualitatively different from a ship or factory but the history of intellectual endeavor proved the opposite.

When science was young and the intricacies of all or most of the known was within the grasp of an individual mind, there was no need for direction, perhaps. Blind wandering over the uncharted tracts of ignorance could lead to wonderful finds by accident.

But as knowledge grew, more and more data had to be absorbed before worthwhile journeys into ignorance could be organized. Men had to specialize. The researcher needed the resources of a library he himself could not gather, then of instruments he himself could not afford.

More and more, the individual researcher gave way to the research team and the research institution.

The funds necessary for research grew greater as tools grew more numerous. What college was so small today as not to require at least one nuclear micro-reactor and at least one three-stage computer?

Centuries before, private individuals could no longer subsidize research. By 1940, only the government, large industries and large universities or research institutions could properly subsidize basic research.

By 1960, even the largest universities depended entirely upon government grants, while research institutions could not exist without tax concessions and public subscriptions. By 2000, the industrial combines had become a branch of the world government and, thereafter, the financing of research and therefore its direction naturally became centralized under a department of the government.

It all worked itself out naturally and well. Every branch of science was fitted neatly to the needs of the public, and the various branches of science were co-ordinated decently. The material advance of the last half century was argument enough for the fact that science was not falling into stagnation.

Foster tried to say a very little of this and was waved aside impatiently by Potterley, who said, "You are parroting official propaganda. You're sitting in the middle of an example that's squarely against the official view. Can you believe that?"

"Frankly, no."

"Well, why do you say time viewing is a dead end? Why is neutrinics unimportant? You say it is. You say it categorically. Yet you've never studied it. You claim complete ignorance of the subject. It's not even given in your school—"

"Isn't the mere fact that it isn't given proof enough?"

"Oh, I see. It's not given because it's unimportant. And

it's unimportant because it's not given. Are you satisfied with that reasoning?"

Foster felt a growing confusion. "It's in the books."

"That's all. The books say neutrinics is unimportant. Your professors tell you so because they read it in the books. The books say so because professors write them. Who says it from personal experience and knowledge? Who does research in it? Do you know of anyone?"

Foster said, "I don't see that we're getting anywhere, Dr. Potterley. I have work to do—"

"One minute. I just want you to try this on. See how it sounds to you. I say the government is actively suppressing basic research in neutrinics and chronoscopy. They're suppressing application of chronoscopy."

"Oh, no."

"Why not? They could do it. There's your centrally directed research. If they refuse grants for research in any portion of science, that portion dies. They've killed neutrinics. They can do it and have done it."

"But why?"

"I don't know why. I want you to find out. I'd do it myself if I knew enough. I came to you because you're a young fellow with a brand-new education. Have your intellectual arteries hardened already? Is there no curiosity in you? Don't you want to *know*? Don't you want *answers?*"

The historian was peering intently into Foster's face. Their noses were only inches apart, and Foster was so lost that he did not think to draw back.

He should, by rights, have ordered Potterley out. If necessary, he should have thrown Potterley out.

It was not respect for age and position that stopped him. It was certainly not that Potterley's arguments had convinced him. Rather, it was a small point of college pride.

Why didn't M.I.T. give a course in neutrinics? For that

matter, now that he came to think of it, he doubted that there was a single book on neutrinics in the library. He could never recall having seen one.

He stopped to think about that.

And that was ruin.

Caroline Potterley had once been an attractive woman. There were occasions, such as dinners or university functions, when, by considerable effort, remnants of the attraction could be salvaged.

On ordinary occasions, she sagged. It was the word she applied to herself in moments of self-abhorrence. She had grown plumper with the years, but the flaccidity about her was not a matter of fat entirely. It was as though her muscles had given up and grown limp so that she shuffled when she walked, while her eyes had grown baggy and her cheeks jowly. Even her graying hair seemed tired rather than merely stringy. Its straightness seemed to be the result of a supine surrender to gravity, nothing else.

Caroline Potterley looked at herself in the mirror and admitted this was one of her bad days. She knew the reason, too.

It had been the dream of Laurel. The strange one, with Laurel grown up. She had been wretched ever since.

Still, she was sorry she had mentioned it to Arnold. He didn't say anything; he never did any more; but it was bad for him. He was particularly withdrawn for days afterward. It might have been that he was getting ready for that important conference with the big government official (he kept saying he expected no success), but it might also have been her dream.

It was better in the old days when he would cry sharply at her, "Let the dead past *go*, Caroline! Talk won't bring her back, and dreams won't either."

It had been bad for both of them. Horribly bad. She had been away from home and had lived in guilt ever since. If she had stayed at home, if she had not gone on an unnecessary shopping expedition, there would have been two of them available. One would have succeeded in saving Laurel.

Poor Arnold had not managed. Heaven knew he tried. He had nearly died himself. He had come out of the burning house, staggering in agony, blistered, choking, half blinded, with the dead Laurel in his arms.

The nightmare of that lived on, never lifting entirely.

Arnold slowly grew a shell about himself afterward. He cultivated a low-voiced mildness through which nothing broke, no lightning struck. He grew puritanical and even abandoned his minor vices, his cigarettes, his penchant for an occasional profane exclamation. He obtained his grant for the preparation of a new history of Carthage and subordinated everything to that.

She tried to help him. She hunted up his references, typed his notes and microfilmed them. Then that ended suddenly.

She ran from the desk suddenly one evening, reaching the bathroom in bare time and retching abominably. Her husband followed her in confusion and concern.

"Caroline, what's wrong?"

It took a drop of brandy to bring her around. She said, "Is it true? What they did?"

"Who did?"

"The Carthaginians."

He stared at her and she got it out by indirection. She couldn't say it right out.

The Carthaginians, it seemed, worshiped Moloch, in the form of a hollow, brazen idol with a furnace in its belly. At times of national crisis, the priests and the people gathered, and infants, after the proper ceremonies and invocations, were dextrously hurled, alive, into the flames.

They were given sweetmeats just before the crucial moment, in order that the efficacy of the sacrifice not be ruined by displeasing cries of panic. The drums rolled just after the moment, to drown out the few seconds of infant shrieking. The parents were present, presumably gratified, for the sacrifice was pleasing to the gods. . . .

Arnold Potterley frowned darkly. Vicious lies, he told her, on the part of Carthage's enemies. He should have warned her. After all, such propagandistic lies were not uncommon. According to the Greeks, the ancient Hebrews worshiped an ass's head in their Holy of Holies. According to the Romans, the primitive Christians were haters of all men who sacrificed pagan children in the catacombs.

"Then they didn't do it?" asked Caroline.

"I'm sure they didn't. The primitive Phoenicians may have. Human sacrifice is commonplace in primitive cultures. But Carthage in her great days was not a primitive culture. Human sacrifice often gives way to symbolic actions such as circumcision. The Greeks and Romans might have mistaken some Carthaginian symbolism for the original full rite, either out of ignorance or out of malice."

"Are you sure?"

"I can't be sure yet, Caroline, but when I've got enough evidence, I'll apply for permission to use chronoscopy, which will settle the matter once and for all."

"Chronoscopy?"

"Time viewing. We can focus on ancient Carthage at some time of crisis, the landing of Scipio Africanus in 202 B.C., for instance, and see with our own eyes exactly what happens. And you'll see, I'll be right."

He patted her and smiled encouragingly, but she dreamed of Laurel every night for two weeks thereafter, and she never helped him with his Carthage project again. Nor did he ever ask her to.

But now she was bracing herself for his coming. He had called her after arriving back in town, told her he had seen the government man and that it had gone as expected. That meant failure, and yet the little telltale sign of depression had been absent from his voice and his features had appeared quite composed in the teleview. He had another errand to take care of, he said, before coming home.

It meant he would be late, but that didn't matter. Neither one of them was particular about eating hours or cared when packages were taken out of the freezer or even which packages, or when the self-warming mechanism was activated.

When he did arrive, he surprised her. There was nothing untoward about him in any obvious way. He kissed her dutifully and smiled, took off his hat and asked if all had been well while he was gone. It was all almost perfectly normal. Almost.

She had learned to detect small things, though, and his pace in all this was a trifle hurried. Enough to show her accustomed eye that he was under tension.

She said, "Has something happened?"

He said, "We're going to have a dinner guest night after next, Caroline. You don't mind?"

"Well, no. Is it anyone I know?"

"No. A young instructor. A newcomer. I've spoken to him." He suddenly whirled toward her and seized her arms at the elbow, held them a moment, then dropped them in confusion as though disconcerted at having shown emotion.

He said, "I almost didn't get through to him. Imagine that. Terrible, *terrible,* the way we have all bent to the yoke; the affection we have for the harness about us."

Mrs. Potterley wasn't sure she understood, but for a year she had been watching him grow quietly more rebellious; little by little more daring in his criticism of the government. She said, "You haven't spoken foolishly to him, have you?"

"What do you mean, foolishly? He'll be doing some neutrinics for me."

"Neutrinics" was trisyllabic nonsense to Mrs. Potterley, but she knew it had nothing to do with history. She said faintly, "Arnold, I don't like you to do that. You'll lose your position. It's—"

"It's intellectual anarchy, my dear," he said. "That's the phrase you want. Very well. I am an anarchist. If the government will not allow me to push my researches, I will push them on my own. And when I show the way, others will follow.... And if they don't, it makes no difference. It's Carthage that counts and human knowledge, not you and I."

"But you don't know this young man. What if he is an agent for the Commission of Research."

"Not likely and I'll take that chance." He made a fist of his right hand and rubbed it gently against the palm of his left. "He's on my side now. I'm sure of it. He can't help but be. I can recognize intellectual curiosity when I see it in a man's eyes and face and attitude, and it's a fatal disease for a tame scientist. Even today it takes time to beat it out of a man and the young ones are vulnerable. ... Oh, why stop at anything? Why not build our own chronoscope and tell the government to go to—"

He stopped abruptly, shook his head and turned away.

"I hope everything will be all right," said Mrs. Potterley, feeling helplessly certain that everything would not be, and frightened, in advance, for her husband's professorial status and the security of their old age.

It was she alone, of them all, who had a violent presentiment of trouble. Quite the wrong trouble, of course.

Jonas Foster was nearly half an hour late in arriving at the Potterleys' off-campus house. Up to that very evening, he had not quite decided he would go. Then, at the last moment, he found he could not bring himself to commit the social enormity of breaking a dinner appointment an hour before the appointed time. That, and the nagging of curiosity.

The dinner itself passed interminably. Foster ate without appetite. Mrs. Potterley sat in distant absentmindedness, emerging out of it only once to ask if he was married and to make a deprecating sound at the news that he was not. Dr. Potterley himself asked neutrally after his professional history and nodded his head primly.

It was as staid, stodgy—boring, actually—as anything could be.

Foster thought: He seems so harmless.

Foster had spent the last two days reading up on Dr. Potterley. Very casually, of course, almost sneakily. He wasn't particularly anxious to be seen in the Social Science Library. To be sure, history was one of those borderline affairs and historical works were frequently read for amusement or edification by the general public.

Still, a physicist wasn't quite the "general public." Let Foster take to reading histories and he would be considered queer, sure as relativity, and after a while the Head of the Department would wonder if his new instructor was really "the man for the job."

So he had been cautious. He sat in the more secluded alcoves and kept his head bent when he slipped in and out at odd hours.

Dr. Potterley, it turned out, had written three books and some dozen articles on the ancient Mediterranean worlds, and the later articles (all in "Historical Reviews") had all dealt with pre-Roman Carthage from a sympathetic viewpoint.

That, at least, checked with Potterley's story and had soothed Foster's suspicions somewhat. ... And yet Foster felt that it would have been much wiser, much safer, to have scotched the matter at the beginning.

A scientist shouldn't be too curious, he thought in bitter dissatisfaction with himself. It's a dangerous trait.

After dinner, he was ushered into Potterley's study and he was brought up sharply at the threshold. The walls were simply lined with books.

Not merely films. There were films, of course, but these were far outnumbered by the books—print on paper. He wouldn't have thought so many books would exist in usable condition.

That bothered Foster. Why should anyone want to keep so many books at home? Surely all were available in the university library, or, at the very worst, at the Library of Congress, if one wished to take the minor trouble of checking out a microfilm.

There was an element of secrecy involved in a home library. It breathed of intellectual anarchy. That last thought, oddly, calmed Foster. He would rather have Potterley be an authentic anarchist than a play-acting *agent provocateur.*

And now the hours began to pass quickly and astonishingly.

"You see," Potterley said, in a clear, unflurried voice, "it was a matter of finding, if possible, anyone who had ever used chronoscopy in his work. Naturally, I couldn't ask baldly, since that would be unauthorized research."

"Yes," said Foster dryly. He was a little surprised such a small consideration would stop the man.

"I used indirect methods—"

He had. Foster was amazed at the volume of correspondence dealing with small disputed points of ancient Mediterranean culture which somehow managed to elicit the casual remark over and over again: "Of course, having never made use of chronoscopy—" or, "Pending approval of my request for chronoscopic data, which appears unlikely at the moment—"

"Now these aren't blind questionings," said Potterley.

"There's a monthly booklet put out by the Institute for Chronoscopy in which items concerning the past as determined by time viewing are printed. Just one or two items.

"What impressed me first was the triviality of most of the items, their insipidity. Why should such researches get priority over my work? So I wrote to people who would be most likely to do research in the directions described in the booklet. Uniformly, as I have shown you, they did *not* make use of the chronoscope. Now let's go over it point by point."

At last Foster, his head swimming with Potterley's meticulously gathered details, asked, "But why?"

"I don't know why," said Potterly, "but I have a theory. The original invention of the chronoscope was by Sterbinski—you see, I know that much—and it was well publicized. But then the government took over the instrument and decided to suppress further research in the matter or any use of the machine. But then, people might be curious as to why it wasn't being used. Curiosity is such a vice, Dr. Foster."

Yes, agreed the physicist to himself.

"Imagine the effectiveness, then," Potterley went on, "of pretending that the chronoscope *was* being used. It would then be not a mystery, but a commonplace. It would no longer be a fitting object for legitimate curiosity or an attractive one for illicit curiosity."

"*You* were curious," pointed out Foster.

Potterley looked a trifle restless. "It was different in my case," he said angrily. "I have something that *must* be done, and I wouldn't submit to the ridiculous way in which they kept putting me off."

A bit paranoid, too, thought Foster gloomily.

Yet he had ended up with something, paranoid or not. Foster could no longer deny that something peculiar was going on in the matter of neutrinics.

But what was Potterley after? That still bothered Foster.

If Potterley didn't intend this as a test of Foster's ethics, what *did* he want?

Foster put it to himself logically. If an intellectual anarchist with a touch of paranoia wanted to use a chronoscope and was convinced that the powers-that-be were deliberately standing in his way, what would he do?

Supposing it were I, he thought. What would I do?

He said slowly, "Maybe the chronoscope doesn't exist at all."

Potterley started. There was almost a crack in his general calmness. For an instant, Foster found himself catching a glimpse of something not at all calm.

But the historian kept his balance and said, "Oh, no, there *must* be a chronoscope."

"Why? Have you seen it? Have I? Maybe that's the explanation of everything. Maybe they're not deliberately holding out on a chronoscope they've got. Maybe they haven't got it in the first place."

"But Sterbinski lived. He built a chronoscope. That much is a fact."

"The books say so," said Foster coldly.

"Now listen." Potterley actually reached over and snatched at Foster's jacket sleeve. "I need the chronoscope. I must have it. Don't tell me it doesn't exist. What we're going to do is find out enough about neutrinics to be able to—"

Potterley drew himself up short.

Foster drew his sleeve away. He needed no ending to that sentence. He supplied it himself. He said, "Build one of our own?"

Potterley looked sour, as though he would rather not have said it point-blank. Nevertheless, he said, "Why not?"

"Because that's out of the question," said Foster. "If what I've read is correct, then it took Sterbinski twenty years to build his machine and several millions in composite grants. Do you think you and I can duplicate that illegally? Suppose we had the time, which we haven't, and suppose I could learn enough out of books, which I doubt, where would we get the money and equipment? The chronoscope is supposed to fill a five-story building, for Heaven's sake."

"Then you won't help me?"

"Well, I'll tell you what. I have one way in which I may be able to find out something—"

"What is that?" asked Potterley at once.

"Never mind. That's not important. But I may be able to find out enough to tell you whether the government is deliberately suppressing research by chronoscope. I may confirm the evidence you already have or I may be able to prove that your evidence is misleading. I don't know what good it will do you in either case, but it's as far as I can go. It's my limit."

Potterley watched the young man go finally. He was angry with himself. Why had he allowed himself to grow so careless as to permit the fellow to guess that he was thinking in terms of a chronoscope of his own? That was premature.

But then why did the young fool have to suppose that a chronoscope might not exist at all?

It *had* to exist. It *had* to. What was the use of saying it didn't?

And why couldn't a second one be built? Science had advanced in the fifty years since Sterbinski. All that was needed was knowledge.

Let the youngster gather knowledge. Let him think a small gathering would be his limit. Having taken the path to anarchy, there would be no limit. If the boy was not driven onward by something in himself, the first steps would be error enough to force the rest. Potterley was quite certain he would not hesitate to use blackmail.

Potterley waved a last good-by and looked up. It was beginning to rain.

Certainly! Blackmail, if necessary, but he would not be stopped.

Foster steered his car across the bleak outskirts of the town and scarcely noticed the rain.

He *was* a fool, he told himself, but he couldn't leave things as they were. He had to know. He damned his streak of undisciplined curiosity, but he had to know.

But he would go no further than Uncle Ralph. He swore mightily to himself that it would stop there. In that way, there would be no evidence against him, no real evidence. Uncle Ralph would be discreet.

In a way, he was secretly ashamed of Uncle Ralph. He hadn't mentioned him to Potterley partly out of caution and partly because he did not wish to witness the lifted eyebrow, the inevitable half-smile. Professional science writers, however useful, were a little outside the pale, fit only for patronizing contempt. The fact that, as a class, they made more money than did research scientists, only made matters worse, of course.

Still, there were times when a science writer in the family could be a convenience. Not being really educated, they did not have to specialize. Consequently, a good science writer knew practically everything. . . . And Uncle Ralph was one of the best.

Ralph Nimmo had no college degree and was rather proud of it. "A degree," he once said to Jonas Foster, when both were considerably younger, "is a first step down a ruinous highway. You don't want to waste it, so you go on to graduate work and doctoral research. You end up a thoroughgoing ignoramus on everything in the world except for one subdivisional sliver of nothing.

"On the other hand, if you guard your mind carefully

and keep it blank of any clutter of information till maturity is reached, filling it only with intelligence and training it only in clear thinking, you then have a powerful instrument at your disposal and you can become a science writer."

Nimmo received his first assignment at the age of twenty-five, after he had completed his apprenticeship and been out in the field for less than three months. It came in the shape of a clotted manuscript whose language would impart no glimmering of understanding to any reader, however qualified, without careful study and some inspired guesswork. Nimmo took it apart and put it together again (after five long and exasperating interviews with the authors, who were biophysicists), making the language taut and meaningful and smoothing the style to a pleasant gloss.

"Why not?" he would say tolerantly to his nephew, who countered his strictures on degrees by berating him with his readiness to hang on the fringes of science. "The fringe is important. Your scientists can't write. Why should they be expected to? They aren't expected to be grand masters at chess or virtuosos at the violin, so why expect them to know how to put words together? Why not leave that for specialists, too?

"Good Lord, Jonas, read your literature of a hundred years ago. Discount the fact that the science is out of date and that some of the expressions are out of date. Just try to read it and make sense out of it. It's just jaw-cracking, amateurish. Papers are published uselessly; whole articles which are either nonsignifant, noncomprehensible, or both."

"But you don't get recognition, Uncle Ralph," protested young Foster, who was getting ready to start his college career and was rather starry-eyed about it. "You could be a terrific researcher."

"I get recognition," said Nimmo. "Don't think for a

minute I don't. Sure, a biochemist or a strato-meteorologist won't give me the time of day, but they pay me well enough. Just find out what happens when some first-class chemist finds the Commission has cut his year's allowance for science writing. He'll fight harder for enough funds to afford me, or someone like me, than to get a recording ionograph."

He grinned broadly, and Foster grinned back. Actually, he was proud of his paunchy, round-faced, stub-fingered uncle, whose vanity made him brush his fringe of hair futilely over the desert on his pate and made him dress like an unmade haystack because such negligence was his trademark. Ashamed, but proud, too.

And now Foster entered his uncle's cluttered apartment in no mood at all for grinning. He was nine years older now and so was Uncle Ralph. For nine more years, papers in every branch of science had come to him for polishing and a little of each had crept into his capacious mind.

Nimmo was eating seedless grapes, popping them into his mouth one at a time. He tossed a bunch to Foster, who caught them by a hair, then bent to retrieve individual grapes that had torn loose and fallen to the floor.

"Let them be. Don't bother," said Nimmo carelessly. "Someone comes in here to clean once a week. What's up? Having trouble with your grant application write-up?"

"I haven't really got into that yet."

"You haven't? Get a move on, boy. Are you waiting for me to offer to do the final arrangement?"

"I couldn't afford you, Uncle."

"Aw, come on. It's all in the family. Grant me all popular publication rights and no cash need change hands."

Foster nodded. "If you're serious, it's a deal."

"It's a deal."

It was a gamble, of course, but Foster knew enough of Nimmo's science writing to realize it could pay off. Some dramatic discovery of public interest on primitive man or on a new surgical technique, or on any branch of spationautics could mean a very cash-attracting article in any of the mass media of communication.

It was Nimmo, for instance, who had written up, for scientific consumption, the series of papers by Bryce and co-workers that elucidated the fine structure of two cancer viruses, for which job he asked the picayune payment of fifteen hundred dollars, provided popular publication rights were included. He then wrote up, exclusively, the same work in semidramatic form for use in trimensional video for a twenty-thousand-dollar advance plus rental royalties that were still coming in after five years.

Foster said bluntly, "What do you know about neutrinics, Uncle?"

"Neutrinics?" Nimmo's small eyes looked surprised. "Are you working in that? I thought it was pseudo-gravitic optics."

"It is p.g.o. I just happen to be asking about neutrinics."

"That's a devil of a thing to be doing. You're stepping out of line. You know that, don't you?"

"I don't expect you to call the Commission because I'm a little curious about things."

"Maybe I should before you get into trouble. Curiosity is an occupational danger with scientists. I've watched it work. One of them will be moving quietly along on a problem, then curiosity leads him up a strange creek. Next thing you know they've done so little on their proper problem, they can't justify for a project renewal. I've seen more—"

"All I want to know," said Foster patiently, "is what's been passing through your hands lately on neutrinics."

Nimmo leaned back, chewing at a grape thoughtfully. "Nothing. Nothing ever. I don't recall ever getting a paper on neutrinics."

"What!" Foster was openly astonished. "Then who does get the work?"

"Now that you ask," said Nimmo, "I don't know. Don't recall anyone talking about it at the annual conventions. I don't think much work is being done there."

"Why not?"

"Hey, there, don't bark. I'm not doing anything. My guess would be—"

Foster was exasperated. "Don't you know?"

"Hmp. I'll tell you what I know about neutrinics. It concerns the applications of neutrino movements and the forces involved—"

"Sure. Sure. Just as electronics deals with the applications of electron movements and the forces involved, and pseudo-gravitics deals with the applications of artificial gravitational fields. I didn't come to you for that. Is that all you know?"

"And," said Nimmo with equanimity, "neutrinics is the basis of time viewing and that *is* all I know."

Foster slouched back in his chair and massaged one lean cheek with great intensity. He felt angrily dissatisfied. Without formulating it explicitly in his own mind, he had felt sure, somehow, that Nimmo would come up with some late reports, bring up interesting facets of modern neutrinics, send him back to Potterley able to say that the elderly historian was mistaken, that his data were misleading, his deductions mistaken.

Then he could have returned to his proper work.

But now . . .

He told himself angrily: So they're not doing much work in the field. Does that make it deliberate suppression? What if neutrinics is a sterile discipline? Maybe it is. I don't know. Potterley doesn't. Why waste the intellectual resources of humanity on nothing? Or the work might be secret for some legitimate reason. It might be . . .

The trouble was, he had to know. He couldn't leave
things as they were now. *He couldn't!*

He said, "Is there a text on neutrinics, Uncle Ralph? I
mean a clear and simple one. An elementary one."

Nimmo thought, his plump cheeks puffing out with a
series of sighs. "You ask the damnedest questions. The
only one I ever heard of was Sterbinski and somebody.
I've never seen it, but I viewed something about it once.
. . . Sterbinski and LaMarr, that's it."

"Is that the Sterbinski who invented the chronoscope?"

"I think so. Proves the book ought to be good."

"Is there a recent edition? Sterbinski died thirty years
ago."

Nimmo shrugged and said nothing.

"Can you find out?"

They sat in silence for a moment, while Nimmo shifted
his bulk to the creaking tune of the chair he sat on. Then
the science writer said, "Are you going to tell me what this
is all about?"

"I can't. Will you help me anyway, Uncle Ralph? Will
you get me a copy of the text?"

"Well, you've taught me all I know on pseudo-gravitics.
I should be grateful. Tell you what—I'll help you on one
condition."

"Which is?"

The older man was suddenly very grave. "That you be
careful, Jonas. You're obviously way out of line, whatever
you're doing. Don't blow up your career just because
you're curious about something you haven't been assigned
to and which is none of your business. Understand?"

Foster nodded, but he hardly heard. He was thinking
furiously.

A full week later, Ralph Nimmo eased his rotund figure
into Jonas Foster's on-campus two-room combination
and said, in a hoarse whisper, "I've got something."

"What?" Foster was immediately eager.

"A copy of Sterbinski and LaMarr." He produced it, or rather a corner of it, from his ample topcoat.

Foster almost automatically eyed door and windows to make sure they were closed and shaded respectively, then held out his hand.

The film case was flaking with age, and when he cracked it the film was faded and growing brittle. He said sharply, "Is this all?"

"Gratitude, my boy, gratitude!" Nimmo sat down with a grunt, and reached into a pocket for an apple.

"Oh, I'm grateful, but it's so old."

"And lucky to get it at that. I tried to get a film run from the Congressional Library. No go. The book was restricted."

"Then how did you get this?"

"Stole it." He was biting crunchingly around the core. "New York Public."

"What?"

"Simple enough. I had access to the stacks, naturally. So I stepped over a chained railing when no one was around, dug this up, and walked out with it. They're very trusting out there. Meanwhile, they won't miss it in years. ... Only you'd better not let anyone see it on you, nephew."

Foster stared at the film as though it were literally hot.

Nimmo discarded the core and reached for a second apple. "Funny thing, now. There's nothing more recent in the whole field of neutrinics. Not a monograph, not a paper, not a progress note. Nothing since the chronoscope."

"Uh-huh," said Foster absently.

Foster worked evenings in the Potterley home. He could not trust his own on-campus rooms for the purpose. The evening work grew more real to him than his own grant applications. Sometimes he worried about it, but then that stopped, too.

His work consisted, at first, simply in viewing and re-viewing the text film. Later it consisted in thinking (some-times while a section of the book ran itself off through the pocket projector, disregarded).

Sometimes Potterley would come down to watch, to sit with prim, eager eyes, as though he expected thought processes to solidify and become visible in all their convo-lutions. He interfered in only two ways. He did not allow Foster to smoke and sometimes he talked.

It wasn't conversation talk, never that. Rather it was a low-voiced monologue with which, it seemed, he scarcely expected to command attention. It was much more as though he were relieving a pressure within himself.

Carthage! Always Carthage!

Carthage, the New York of the ancient Mediterranean. Carthage, commercial empire and queen of the seas. Car-thage, all that Syracuse and Alexandria pretended to be. Carthage, maligned by her enemies and inarticulate in her own defense.

She had been defeated once by Rome and then driven out of Sicily and Sardinia, but came back to more than recoup her losses by new dominions in Spain, and raised up Hannibal to give the Romans sixteen years of terror.

In the end, she lost again a second time, reconciled herself to fate and built again with broken tools a limping life in shrunken territory, succeeding so well that jealous Rome deliberately forced a third war. And then Carthage, with nothing but bare hands and tenacity, built weapons and forced Rome into a two-year war that ended only with complete destruction of the city, the inhabitants throwing themselves into their flaming houses rather than surrender.

"Could people fight so for a city and a way of life as bad as the ancient writers painted it? Hannibal was a better general than any Roman and his soldiers were absolutely faithful to him. Even his bitterest enemies praised him. There was a Carthaginian. It is fashionable to say that he was an atypical Carthaginian, better than the others, a diamond placed in garbage. But then why was he so faithful to Carthage, even to his death after years of exile? They talk of Moloch—"

Foster didn't always listen, but sometimes he couldn't help himself and he shuddered and turned sick at the bloody tale of child sacrifice.

But Potterley went on earnestly, "Just the same, it isn't true. It's a twenty-five-hundred-year-old canard started by the Greeks and Romans. They had their own slaves, their crucifixions and torture, their gladiatorial contests. They weren't holy. The Moloch story is what later ages would have called war propaganda, the big lie. I can prove it was a lie. I can prove it and, by Heaven, I will—I will—"

He would mumble that promise over and over again in his earnestness.

Mrs. Potterley visited him also, but less frequently, usually on Tuesdays and Thursdays, when Dr. Potterley himself had an evening course to take care of and was not present.

She would sit quietly, scarcely talking, face slack and doughy, eyes blank, her whole attitude distant and withdrawn.

The first time, Foster tried, uneasily, to suggest that she leave.

She said tonelessly, "Do I disturb you?"

"No, of course not," lied Foster restlessly. "It's just that—that—" He couldn't complete the sentence.

She nodded, as though accepting an invitation to stay. Then she opened a cloth bag she had brought with her and took out a quire of vitron sheets which she proceeded to weave together by rapid, delicate movements of a pair of slender, tetra-faceted depolarizers, whose battery-fed wires made her look as though she were holding a large spider.

One evening, she said softly, "My daughter, Laurel, is your age."

Foster started, as much at the sudden unexpected sound of speech as at the words. He said, "I didn't know you had a daughter, Mrs. Potterley."

"She died. Years ago."

The vitron grew under the deft manipulations into the uneven shape of some garment Foster could not yet identify. There was nothing left for him to do but mutter inanely, "I'm sorry."

Mrs. Potterley sighed. "I dream about her often." She raised her blue, distant eyes to him.

Foster winced and looked away.

Another evening she asked, pulling at one of the vitron sheets to loosen its gentle clinging to her dress, "What is time viewing anyway?"

That remark broke into a particularly involved chain of thought, and Foster said snappishly, "Dr. Potterley can explain."

"He's tried to. Oh, my, yes. But I think he's a little impatient with me. He calls it chronoscopy most of the time. Do you actually see things in the past, like the trimensionals? Or does it just make little dot patterns like the computer you use?"

Foster stared as his hand computer with distaste. It worked well enough, but every operation had to be manually controlled and the answers were obtained in code. Now if he could use the school computer ... Well, why dream, he felt conspicuous enough, as it was, carrying a hand computer under his arm every evening as he left his office.

He said, "I've never seen the chronoscope myself, but

I'm under the impression that you actually see pictures and hear sound."

"You can hear people talk, too?"

"I think so." Then, half in desperation, "Look here, Mrs. Potterley, this must be awfully dull for you. I realize you don't like to leave a guest all to himself, but really, Mrs. Potterley, you mustn't feel compelled—"

"I don't feel compelled," she said. "I'm sitting here, waiting."

"Waiting? For what?"

She said composedly, "I listened to you that first evening. The time you first spoke to Arnold. I listened at the door."

He said, "You did?"

"I know I shouldn't have, but I was awfully worried about Arnold. I had a notion he was going to do something he oughtn't and I wanted to hear what. And then when I heard—" She paused, bending close over the vitron and peering at it.

"Heard what, Mrs. Potterley?"

"That you wouldn't build a chronoscope."

"Well, of course not."

"I thought maybe you might change your mind."

Foster glared at her. "Do you mean you're coming down here hoping I'll build a chronoscope, waiting for me to build one?"

"I hope you do, Dr. Foster. Oh, I hope you do."

It was as though, all at once, a fuzzy veil had fallen off her face, leaving all her features clear and sharp, putting color into her cheeks, life into her eyes, the vibrations of something approaching excitement into her voice.

"Wouldn't it be wonderful," she whispered, "to have one? People of the past could live again. Pharoahs and kings and—just people. I hope you build one, Dr. Foster. I really—hope—"

She choked, it seemed, on the intensity of her own

words and let the vitron sheets slip off her lap. She rose and ran up the basement stairs, while Foster's eyes followed her awkwardly fleeing body with astonishment and distress.

It cut deeper into Foster's nights and left him sleepless and painfully stiff with thought. It was almost a mental indigestion.

His grant requests went limping in, finally, to Ralph Nimmo. He scarcely had any hope for them. He thought numbly: They won't be approved.

If they weren't, of course, it would create a scandal in the department and probably mean his appointment at the university would not be renewed, come the end of the academic year.

He scarcely worried. It was the neutrino, the neutrino, only the neutrino. Its trail curved and veered sharply and led him breathlessly along uncharted pathways that even Sterbinski and LaMarr did not follow.

He called Nimmo. "Uncle Ralph, I need a few things. I'm calling from off the campus."

Nimmo's face in the video plate was jovial, but his voice was sharp. He said, "What you need is a course in communication. I'm having a hell of a time pulling your application into one intelligible piece. If that's what you're calling about—"

Foster shook his head impatiently. "That's *not* what I'm calling about. I need these." He scribbled quickly on a piece of paper and held it up before the receiver.

Nimmo yiped. "Hey, how many tricks do you think I can wangle?"

"You can get them, Uncle. You know you can."

Nimmo reread the list of items with silent motions of his plump lips and looked grave.

"What happens when you put those things together?" he asked.

Foster shook his head. "You'll have exclusive popular

publication rights to whatever turns up, the way it's always been. But please don't ask any questions now."

"I can't do miracles, you know."

"Do this one. You've got to. You're a science writer, not a research man. You don't have to account for anything. You've got friends and connections. They can look the other way, can't they, to get a break from you next publication time?"

"Your faith, nephew, is touching. I'll try."

Nimmo succeeded. The material and equipment were brought over late one evening in a private touring car. Nimmo and Foster lugged it in with the grunting of men unused to manual labor.

Potterley stood at the entrance of the basement after Nimmo had left. He asked softly, "What's this for?"

Foster brushed the hair off his forehead and gently massaged a sprained wrist. He said, "I want to conduct a few simple experiments."

"Really?" The historian's eyes glittered with excitement.

Foster felt exploited. He felt as though he were being led along a dangerous highway by the pull of pinching fingers on his nose; as though he could see the ruin clearly that lay in wait at the end of the path, yet walked eagerly and determinedly. Worst of all, he felt the compelling grip on his nose to be his own.

It was Potterley who began it, Potterley who stood there now, gloating; but the compulsion was his own.

Foster said sourly, "I'll be wanting privacy now, Potterley. I can't have you and your wife running down here and annoying me."

He thought: If that offends him, let him kick me out. Let him put an end to this.

In his heart, though, he did not think being evicted would stop anything.

But it did not come to that. Potterley was showing no

signs of offense. His mild gaze was unchanged. He said, "Of course, Dr. Foster, of course. All the privacy you wish."

Foster watched him go. He was left still marching along the highway, perversely glad of it and hating himself for being glad.

He took to sleeping over on a cot in Potterley's basement and spending his weekends there entirely.

During that period, preliminary word came through that his grants (as doctored by Nimmo) had been approved. The Department Head brought the word and congratulated him.

Foster stared back distantly and mumbled, "Good. I'm glad," with so little conviction that the other frowned and turned away without another word.

Foster gave the matter no further thought. It was a minor point, worth no notice. He was planning something that really counted, a climactic test for that evening.

One evening, a second and third and then, haggard and half beside himself with excitement, he called in Potterley.

Potterley came down the stairs and looked about at the homemade gadgetry. He said, in his soft voice, "The electric bills are quite high. I don't mind the expense, but the City may ask questions. Can anything be done?"

It was a warm evening, but Potterley wore a tight collar and a semijacket. Foster, who was in his undershirt, lifted bleary eyes and said shakily, "It won't be for much longer, Dr. Potterley. I've called you down to tell you something. A chronoscope can be built. A small one, of course, but it can be built."

Potterley seized the railing. His body sagged. He managed a whisper. "Can it be built here?"

"Here in the basement," said Foster wearily.

"Good Lord. You said—"

"I know what I said," cried Foster impatiently. "I said

it couldn't be done. I didn't know anything then. Even Sterbinski didn't know anything."

Potterley shook his head. "Are you sure? You're not mistaken, Dr. Foster? I couldn't endure it if—"

Foster said, "I'm not mistaken. Damn it, sir, if just theory had been enough, we could have had a time viewer over a hundred years ago, when the neutrino was first postulated. The trouble was, the original investigators considered it only a mysterious particle without mass or charge that could not be detected. It was just something to even up the bookkeeping and save the law of conservation of mass energy."

He wasn't sure Potterley knew what he was talking about. He didn't care. He needed a breather. He had to get some of this out of his clotting thoughts. . . . And he needed background for what he would have to tell Potterley next.

He went on. "It was Sterbinski who first discovered that the neutrino broke through the space-time cross-sectional barrier, that it traveled through time as well as through space. It was Sterbinski who first devised a method for stopping neutrinos. He invented a neutrino recorder and learned how to interpret the pattern of the neutrino stream. Naturally, the stream had been affected and deflected by all the matter it had passed through in its passage through time, and the deflections could be analyzed and converted into the images of the matter that had done the deflecting. Time viewing was possible. Even air vibrations could be detected in this way and converted into sound."

Potterley was definitely not listening. He said, "Yes. Yes. But when can you build a chronoscope?"

Foster said urgently, "Let me finish. Everything depends on the method used to detect and analyze the neutrino stream. Sterbinski's method was difficult and roundabout. It required mountains of energy. But I've

studied pseudo-gravitics, Dr. Potterley, the science of artificial gravitational fields. I've specialized in the behavior
of light in such fields. It's a new science. Sterbinski knew
nothing of it. If he had, he would have seen—anyone
would have—a much better and more efficient method of
detecting neutrinos using a pseudo-gravitic field. If I had
known more neutrinics to begin with, I would have seen it
at once."

Potterley brightened a bit. "I knew it," he said. "Even if
they stop research in neutrinics there is no way the government can be sure that discoveries in other segments of
science won't reflect knowledge on neutrinics. So much
for the value of centralized direction of science. I thought
this long ago, Dr. Foster, before you ever came to work
here."

"I congratulate you on that," said Foster, "but there's
one thing—"

"Oh, never mind all this. Answer me. Please. When can
you build a chronoscope?"

"I'm trying to tell you something, Dr. Potterley. A
chronoscope won't do you any good." (This is it, Foster
thought.)

Slowly, Potterley descended the stairs. He stood facing
Foster. "What do you mean? Why won't it help me?"

"You won't see Carthage. It's what I've got to tell you.
It's what I've been leading up to. You can never see
Carthage."

Potterley shook his head slightly. "Oh, no, you're
wrong. If you have the chronoscope, just focus it properly—"

"No, Dr. Potterley. It's not a question of focus. There
are random factors affecting the neutrino stream, as they
affect all subatomic particles. What we call the uncertainty principle. When the stream is recorded and inter-
preted, the random factor comes out as fuzziness, or
'noise,' as the communications boys speak of it. The far-

ther back in time you penetrate, the more pronounced the fuzziness, the greater the noise. After a while, the noise drowns out the picture. Do you understand?"

"More power," said Potterley in a dead kind of voice.

"That won't help. When the noise blurs out detail, magnifying detail magnifies the noise, too. You can't see anything in a sun-burned film by enlarging it, can you? Get this through your head, now. The physical nature of the universe sets limits. The random thermal motions of air molecules set limits to how weak a sound can be detected by any instrument. The length of a light wave or of an electron wave sets limits to the size of objects that can be seen by any instrument. It works that way in chronoscopy, too. You can only time view so far."

"How far? How far?"

Foster took a deep breath. "A century and a quarter. That's the most."

"But the monthly bulletin the Commission puts out deals with ancient history almost entirely." The historian laughed shakily. "You must be wrong. The government has data as far back as 3000 B.C."

"When did you switch to believing them?" demanded Foster, scornfully. "You began this business by proving they were lying; that no historian had made use of the chronoscope. Don't you see why now? No historian, except one interested in contemporary history, could. No chronoscope can possibly see back in time farther than 1920 under any conditions."

"You're wrong. You don't know everything," said Potterley.

"The truth won't bend itself to your convenience either. Face it. The government's part in this is to perpetuate a hoax."

"Why?"

"I don't know why."

Potterley's snubby nose was twitching. His eyes were

bulging. He pleaded, "It's only theory, Dr. Foster. Build a chronoscope. Build one and try."

Foster caught Potterley's shoulders in a sudden, fierce grip. "Do you think I haven't? Do you think I would tell you this before I had checked it every way I knew? I *have* built one. It's all around you. Look!"

He ran to the switches at the power leads. He flicked them on, one by one. He turned a resistor, adjusted other knobs, put out the cellar lights. "Wait. Let it warm up."

There was a small glow near the center of one wall. Potterley was gibbering incoherently, but Foster only cried again, "Look!"

The light sharpened and brightened, broke up into a light-and-dark pattern. Men and women! Fuzzy. Features blurred. Arms and legs mere streaks. An old-fashioned ground car, unclear but recognizable as one of the kind that had once used gasoline-powered internal-combustion engines, sped by.

Foster said, "Mid-twentieth century, somewhere. I can't hook up an audio yet, so this is soundless. Eventually, we can add sound. Anyway, mid-twentieth is almost as far back as you can go. Believe me, that's the best focusing that can be done."

Potterley said, "Build a larger machine, a stronger one. Improve your circuits."

"You can't lick the Uncertainty Principle, man, any more than you can live on the sun. There are physical limits to what can be done."

"You're lying. I won't believe you. I—"

A new voice sounded, raised shrilly to make itself heard.

"Arnold! Dr. Foster!"

The young physicist turned at once. Dr. Potterley froze for a long moment, then said, without turning, "What is it, Caroline? Leave us."

"No!" Mrs. Potterley descended the stairs. "I heard. I

couldn't help hearing. Do you have a time viewer here, Dr. Foster? Here in the basement?"

"Yes, I do, Mrs. Potterley. A kind of time viewer. Not a good one. I can't get sound yet and the picture is darned blurry, but it works."

Mrs. Potterley clasped her hands and held them tightly against her breast. "How wonderful. How wonderful."

"It's not at all wonderful," snapped Potterley. "The young fool can't reach farther back than—"

"Now, look," began Foster in exasperation . . .

"Please!" cried Mrs. Potterley. "Listen to me. Arnold, don't you see that as long as we can use it for twenty years back, we can see Laurel once again? What do we care about Carthage and ancient times? It's Laurel we can see. She'll be alive for us again. Leave the machine here, Dr. Foster. Show us how to work it."

Foster stared at her, then at her husband. Dr. Potterley's face had gone white. Though his voice stayed low and even, its calmness was somehow gone. He said, "You're a fool!"

Caroline said weakly, "Arnold!"

"You're a fool, I say. What will you see? The past. The dead past. Will Laurel do one thing she did not do? Will you see one thing you haven't seen? Will you live three years over and over again, watching a baby who'll never grow up, no matter how you watch?"

His voice came near to cracking, but held. He stopped closer to her, seized her shoulder and shook her roughly. "Do you know what will happen to you if you do that? They'll come to take you away because you'll go mad. Yes, mad. Do you want mental treatment? Do you want to be shut up, to undergo the psychic probe?"

Mrs. Potterley tore away. There was no trace of softness or vagueness about her. She had twisted into a virago. "I want to see my child, Arnold. She's in that machine and I want her."

"She's *not* in the machine. An image is. Can't you understand? An image! Something that's not real!"

"I want my child. Do you hear me?" She flew at him, screaming, fists beating. *"I want my child."*

The historian retreated at the fury of the assault, crying out. Foster moved to step between, when Mrs. Potterley dropped, sobbing wildly, to the floor.

Potterley turned, eyes desperately seeking. With a sudden heave, he snatched at a Lando-rod, tearing it from its support, and whirling away before Foster, numbed by all that was taking place, could move to stop him.

"Stand back!" gasped Potterley, "or I'll kill you. I swear it."

He swung with force, and Foster jumped back.

Potterley turned with fury on every part of the structure in the cellar, and Foster, after the first crash of glass, watched dazedly.

Potterley spent his rage and then he was standing quietly amid shards and splinters, with a broken Lando-rod in his hand. He said to Foster in a whisper, "Now get out of here! Never come back! If any of this cost you anything, send me a bill and I'll pay for it. I'll pay double."

Foster shrugged, picked up his shirt and moved up the basement stairs. He could hear Mrs. Potterley sobbing loudly, and as he turned at the head of the stairs for a last look, he saw Dr. Potterley bending over her, his face convulsed with sorrow.

Two days later, with the school day drawing to a close and Foster looking wearily about to see if there was any data on his newly approved projects that he wished to take home, Dr. Potterley appeared once more. He was standing at the open door of Foster's office.

The historian was neatly dressed as ever. He lifted his hand in a gesture that was too vague to be a greeting, too abortive to be a plea. Foster stared stonily.

Potterley said, "I waited till five, till you were . . . May I come in?"

Foster nodded.

Potterley said, "I suppose I ought to apologize for my behavior. I was dreadfully disappointed; not quite master of myself. Still, it was inexcusable."

"I accept your apology," said Foster. "Is that all?"

"My wife called you, I think."

"Yes, she has."

"She has been quite hysterical. She told me she had, but I couldn't be quite sure—"

"Could you tell me—would you be so kind as to tell me what she wanted?"

"She wanted a chronoscope. She said she had some money of her own. She was willing to pay."

"Did you—make any commitments?"

"I said I wasn't in the manufacturing business."

"Good," breathed Potterley, his chest expanding with a sigh of relief. "Please don't take any calls from her. She's not—quite—"

"Look, Dr. Potterley," said Foster, "I'm not getting into any domestic quarrels, but you'd better be prepared for something. Chronoscopes can be built by anybody. Given a few simple parts that can be bought through some etherics sales center, it can be built in the home workshop. The video part, anyway."

"But no one else will think of it beside you, will they? No one has."

"I don't intend to keep it secret."

"But you can't publish. It's illegal research."

"That doesn't matter any more, Dr. Potterley. If I lose my grants, I lose them. If the university is displeased, I'll resign. It just doesn't matter."

"But you can't do that!"

"Till now," said Foster, "you didn't mind my risking loss of grants and position. Why do you turn so tender about it now? Now let me explain something to you. When you first came to me, I believed in organized and directed research; the situation as it existed, in other words. I considered you an intellectual anarchist, Dr. Potterley, and dangerous. But, for one reason or another, I've been an anarchist myself for months now and I have achieved great things.

"Those things have been achieved not because I am a brilliant scientist. Not at all. It was just that scientific research had been directed from above and holes were left that could be filled in by anyone who looked in the right direction. And anyone might have if the government hadn't actively tried to prevent it.

"Now understand me. I still believe directed research can be useful. I'm not in favor of a retreat to total anarchy. But there must be a middle ground. Directed research can retain flexibility. A scientist must be allowed to follow his curiosity, at least in his spare time."

Potterley sat down. He said ingratiatingly, "Let's discuss this, Foster. I appreciate your idealism. You're young. You want the moon. But you can't destroy yourself through fancy notions of what research must consist of. I got you into this. I am responsible and I blame myself bitterly. I was acting emotionally. My interest in Carthage blinded me and I was a damned fool."

Foster broke in. "You mean you've changed completely in two days? Carthage is nothing? Government suppression of research is nothing?"

"Even a damned fool like myself can learn, Foster. My wife taught me something. I understand the reason for government suppression of neutrinics now. I didn't two days ago. And, understanding, I approve. You saw the way my wife reacted to the news of a chronoscope in the basement. I had envisioned a chronoscope used for research purposes. All *she* could see was the personal pleasure of returning neurotically to a personal past, a dead past. The pure researcher, Foster, is in the minority. People like my wife would outweigh us.

"For the government to encourage chronoscopy would have meant that everyone's past would be visible. The government officers would be subjected to blackmail and improper pressure, since who on Earth has a past that is absolutely clean? Organized government might become impossible."

Foster licked his lips. "Maybe. Maybe the government has some justification in its own eyes. Still, there's an important principle involved here. Who knows what other scientific advances are being stymied because scientists are being stifled into walking a narrow path? If the chronoscope becomes the terror of a few politicians, it's a price that must be paid. The public must realize that science must be free and there is no more dramatic way of doing it than to publish my discovery, one way or another, legally or illegally."

Potterley's brow was damp with perspiration, but his voice remained even. "Oh, not just a few politicians, Dr. Foster. Don't think that. It would be my terror, too. My wife would spend her time living with our dead daughter. She would retreat further from reality. She would go mad living the same scenes over and over. And not just my terror. There would be others like her. Children searching for their dead parents or their own youth. We'll have a whole world living in the past. Midsummer madness."

Foster said, "Moral judgments can't stand in the way. There isn't one advance at any time in history that mankind hasn't had the ingenuity to pervert. Mankind must also have the ingenuity to prevent. As for the chronoscope, your delvers into the dead past will get tired soon enough. They'll catch their loved parents in some of the things their loved parents did and they'll lose their enthusiasm for it all. But all this is trivial. With me, it's a matter of important principle."

Potterley said,"Hang your principle. Can't you understand men and women as well as principle? Don't you
understand that my wife will live through the fire that
killed our baby? She won't be able to help herself. I know
her. She'll follow through each step, trying to prevent it.
She'll live it over and over again, hoping each time that it
won't happen. How many times do you want to kill Laurel?" A huskiness had crept into his voice.

A thought crossed Foster's mind. "What are you really
afraid she'll find out, Dr. Potterley? What happened the
night of the fire?"

The historian's hands went up quickly to cover his face
and they shook with his dry sobs. Foster turned away and
stared uncomfortably out the window.

Potterley said after a while, "It's a long time since I've
had to think of it. Caroline was away. I was baby-sitting. I
went into the baby's bedroom mid-evening to see if she
had kicked off the bedclothes. I had my cigarette with me.
. . . I smoked in those days. I must have stubbed it out
before putting it in the ashtray on the chest of drawers. I
was always careful. The baby was all right. I returned to
the living room and fell asleep before the video. I awoke,
choking, surrounded by fire. I don't know how it started."

"But you think it may have been the cigarette, is that
it?" said Foster. "A cigarette which, for once, you forgot
to stub out?"

"I don't know. I tried to save her, but she was dead in
my arms when I got out."

"You never told your wife about the cigarette, I suppose."

Potterley shook his head. "But I've lived with it."

"Only now, with a chronoscope, she'll find out. Maybe
it wasn't the cigarette. Maybe you did stub it out. Isn't
that possible?"

The scant tears had dried on Potterley's face. The red-
ness had subsided. He said, "I can't take the chance. . . .

But it's not just myself, Foster. The past has its terrors for most people. Don't loose those terrors on the human race."

Foster paced the floor. Somehow, this explained the reason for Potterley's rabid, irrational desire to boost the Carthaginians, deify them, most of all disprove the story of their fiery sacrifices to Moloch. By freeing them of the guilt of infanticide by fire, he symbolically freed himself of the same guilt.

So the same fire that had driven him on to causing the construction of a chronoscope was now driving him on to the destruction.

Foster looked sadly at the older man. "I see your position, Dr. Potterley, but this goes above personal feelings. I've got to smash this throttling hold on the throat of science."

Potterley said, savagely, "You mean you want the fame and wealth that goes with such a discovery."

"I don't know about the wealth, but that, too, I suppose. I'm no more than human."

"You won't suppress your knowledge?"

"Not under any circumstances."

"Well, then—" And the historian got to his feet and stood for a moment, glaring.

Foster had an odd moment of terror. The man was older than he, smaller, feebler, and he didn't look armed. Still . . .

Foster said, "If you're thinking of killing me or anything insane like that, I've got the information in a safety-deposit vault where the proper people will find it in case of my disappearance or death."

Potterley said, "Don't be a fool," and stalked out.

Foster closed the door, locked it and sat down to think. He felt silly. He had no information in any safety-deposit vault, of course. Such a melodramatic action would not have occurred to him ordinarily. But now it had.

Feeling even sillier, he spent an hour writing out the equations of the application of pseudo-gravitic optics to neutrinic recording, and some diagrams for the engineering details of construction. He sealed it in an envelope and scrawled Ralph Nimmo's name over the outside.

He spent a rather restless night and the next morning, on the way to school, dropped the envelope off at the bank, with appropriate instructions to an official, who made him sign a paper permitting the box to be opened after his death.

He called Nimmo to tell him of the existence of the envelope, refusing querulously to say anything about its contents.

He had never felt so ridiculously self-conscious as at that moment.

That night and the next, Foster spent in only fitful sleep, finding himself face to face with the highly practical problem of the publication of data unethically obtained.

The *Proceedings of the Society for Pseudo-Gravitics,* which was the journal with which he was best acquainted, would certainly not touch any paper that did not include the magic footnote: "The work described in this paper was made possible by Grant No. So-and-So from the Commision of Research of the United Nations."

Nor, doubly so, would the *Journal of Physics.*

There were always the minor journals who might overlook the nature of the article for the sake of the sensation, but that would require a little financial negotiation on which he hesitated to embark. It might, on the whole, be better to pay the cost of publishing a small pamphlet for general distribution among scholars. In that case, he would even be able to dispense with the services of a science writer, sacrificing polish for speed. He would have to find a reliable printer. Uncle Ralph might know one.

He walked down the corridor to his office and wondered anxiously if perhaps he ought to waste no further time, give himself no further chance to lapse into indecision and take the risk of calling Ralph from his office phone. He was so absorbed in his own heavy thoughts that he did not notice that his room was occupied until he turned from the clothes closet and approached his desk.

Dr. Potterley was there and a man whom Foster did not recognize.

Foster stared at them. "What's this?"

Potterley said, "I'm sorry, but I had to stop you."

Foster continued staring. "What are you talking about?"

The stranger said, "Let me introduce myself." He had large teeth, a little uneven, and they showed prominently when he smiled. "I am Thaddeus Araman, Department Head of the Division of Chronoscopy. I am here to see you concerning information brought to me by Professor Arnold Potterley and confirmed by our own sources—"

Potterley said breathlessly, "I took all the blame, Dr. Foster. I explained that it was I who persuaded you against your will into unethical practices. I have offered to accept full responsibility and punishment. I don't wish you harmed in any way. It's just that chronoscopy must not be permitted!"

Araman nodded. "He had taken the blame as he says, Dr. Foster, but this thing is out of his hands now."

Foster said, "So? What are you going to do? Blackball me from all consideration for research grants?"

"That is in my power," said Araman.

"Order the university to discharge me?"

"That, too, is in my power."

"All right, go ahead. Consider it done. I'll leave my office now, with you. I can send for my books later. If you insist, I'll leave my books. Is that all?"

"Not quite," said Araman. "You must engage to do no further research in chronoscopy, to publish none of your findings in chronoscopy and, of course, to build no chronoscope. You will remain under surveillance indefinitely to make sure you keep that promise."

"Supposing I refuse to promise? What can you do? Doing research out of my field may be unethical, but it isn't a criminal offense."

"In the case of chronoscopy, my young friend," said Araman patiently, "it is a criminal offense. If necessary, you will be put in jail and kept there."

"Why?" shouted Foster. "What's magic about chronoscopy?"

Araman said, "That's the way it is. We cannot allow further developments in the field. My own job is, primarily, to make sure of that, and I intend to do my job. Unfortunately, I had no knowledge, nor did anyone in the department, that the optics of pseudo-gravity fields had such immediate application to chronoscopy. Score one for general ignorance, but henceforward research will be steered properly in that respect, too."

Foster said, "That won't help. Something else may apply that neither you nor I dream of. All science hangs together. It's one piece. If you want to stop one part, you've got to stop it all."

"No doubt that is true," said Araman, "in theory. On the practical side, however, we have managed quite well to hold chronoscopy down to the original Sterbinski level for fifty years. Having caught you in time, Dr. Foster, we hope to continue doing so indefinitely. And we wouldn't have come this close to disaster, either, if I had accepted Dr. Potterley at something more than face value."

He turned toward the historian and lifted his eyebrows in a kind of humorous self-deprecation. "I'm afraid, sir, that I dismissed you as a history professor and no more on the occasion of our first interview. Had I done my job properly and checked on you, this would not have happened."

Foster said abruptly, "Is anyone allowed to use the government chronoscope?"

"No one outside our division under any pretext. I say that since it is obvious to me that you have already guessed as much. I warn you, though, that any repetition of that fact will be a criminal, not an ethical, offense."

"And your chronoscope doesn't go back more than a hundred twenty-five years or so, does it?"

"It doesn't."

"Then your bulletin with its stories of time viewing ancient times is a hoax?"

Araman said coolly, "With the knowledge you now have, it is obvious you know that for a certainty. However, I confirm your remark. The monthly bulletin is a hoax."

"In that case," said Foster, "I will not promise to suppress my knowledge of chronoscopy. If you wish to arrest me, go ahead. My defense at the trial will be enough to destroy the vicious card house of directed research and bring it tumbling down. Directing research is one thing; suppressing it and depriving mankind of its benefits is quite another."

Araman said, "Oh, let's get something straight, Dr. Foster. If you do not co-operate, you will go to jail directly. You will *not* see a lawyer, you will *not* be charged, you will *not* have a trial. You will simply stay in jail."

"Oh, no," said Foster, "you're bluffing. This is not the twentieth century, you know."

There was a stir outside the office, the clatter of feet, a high-pitched shout that Foster was sure he recognized. The door crashed open, the lock splintering, the three intertwined figures stumbled in.

As they did so, one of the men raised a blaster and brought its butt down hard on the skull of another.

There was a whoosh of expiring air, and the one whose head had been struck went limp.

"Uncle Ralph!" cried Foster.

Araman frowned. "Put him down in that chair," he ordered, "and get some water."

Ralph Nimmo, rubbing his head with a gingerly sort of disgust, said, "There was no need to get rough, Araman."

Araman said, "The guard should have been rough sooner and kept you out of here, Nimmo. You'd have been better off."

"You know each other?" asked Foster.

"I've had dealings with the man," said Nimmo, still rubbing. "If he's here in your office, nephew, you're in trouble."

"And you, too," said Araman angrily. "I know Dr. Foster consulted you on neutrinics literature."

Nimmo corrugated his forehead, then straightened it with a wince as though the action had brought pain. "So?" he said. "What else do you know about me?"

"We will know everything about you soon enough. Meanwhile, that one item is enough to implicate you. What are you doing here?"

"My dear Dr. Araman," said Nimmo, some of his jauntiness restored, "day before yesterday, my jackass of a nephew called me. He had placed some mysterious information—"

"Don't tell him! Don't say anything!" cried Foster.

Araman glanced at him coldly. "We know all about it, Dr. Foster. The safety-deposit box has been opened and its contents removed."

"But how can you know—" Foster's voice died away in a kind of furious frustration.

"Anyway," said Nimmo, "I decided the net must be closing around him and, after I took care of a few items, I came down to tell him to get off this thing he's doing. It's not worth his career."

"Does that mean you know what he's doing?" asked Araman.

"He never told me," said Nimmo, "but I'm a science writer with a hell of a lot of experience. I know which side of an atom is electronified. The boy, Foster, specializes in pseudo-gravitic optics and coached me on the stuff himself. He got me to get him a textbook on neutrinics and I kind of ship-viewed it myself before handing it over. I can put the two together. He asked me to get him certain pieces of physical equipment, and that was evidence, too. Stop me if I'm wrong, but my nephew has built a semi-portable, low-power chronoscope. Yes, or—yes?"

"Yes." Araman reached thoughtfully for a cigarette and paid no attention to Dr. Potterley (watching silently, as though all were a dream), who shied away, gasping, from the white cylinder. "Another mistake for me. I ought to resign. I should have put tabs on you, too, Nimmo, instead of concentrating too hard on Potterley and Foster. I didn't have much time, of course, and you've ended up safely here, but that doesn't excuse me. You're under arrest, Nimmo."

"What for?" demanded the science writer.

"Unauthorized research."

"I wasn't doing any. I can't, not being a registered scientist. And even if I did, it's not a criminal offense."

Foster said savagely, "No use, Uncle Ralph. This bureaucrat is making his own laws."

"Like what?" demanded Nimmo.

"Like life imprisonment without trial."

"Nuts," said Nimmo. "This isn't the twentieth cen——"

"I tried that," said Foster. "It doesn't bother him."

"Well, nuts," shouted Nimmo. "Look here, Araman. My nephew and I have relatives who haven't lost touch with us, you know. The professor has some also, I imagine. You can't just make us disappear. There'd be questions and a scandal. This *isn't* the twentieth century. So if you're trying to scare us, it isn't working."

The cigarette snapped between Araman's fingers and he

tossed it away violently. He said, "Damn it, I don't know *what* to do. It's never been like this before. . . . Look! You three fools know nothing of what you're trying to do. You understand nothing. Will you listen to me?"

"Oh, we'll listen," said Nimmo grimly.

(Foster sat silently, eyes angry, lips compressed. Potterley's hands writhed like two intertwined snakes.)

Araman said, "The past to you is the dead past. If any of you have discussed the matter, it's dollars to nickels you've used that phrase. The dead past. If you knew how many times I've heard those three words, you'd choke on them, too.

"When people think of the past, they think of it as dead, far away and gone, long ago. We encourage them to think so. When we report time viewing, we always talk of views centuries in the past, even though you gentlemen know seeing more than a century or so is impossible. People accept it. The past means Greece, Rome, Carthage, Egypt, the Stone Age. The deader, the better.

"Now you three know a century or a little more is the limit, so what does the past mean to you? Your youth. Your first girl. Your dead mother. Twenty years ago. Thirty years ago. Fifty years ago. The deader, the better. . . . But when does the past really begin?"

He paused in anger. The others stared at him and Nimmo stirred uneasily.

"Well," said Araman, "when did it begin? A year ago? Five minutes ago? One second ago? Isn't it obvious that the past begins an instant ago? The dead past is just another name for the living present. What if you focus the chronoscope in the past of one-hundredth of a second ago? Aren't you watching the present? Does it begin to sink in?"

Nimmo said, "Damnation."

"Damnation," mimicked Araman. "After Potterley came to me with his story night before last, how do you suppose I checked up on both of you? I did it with the chronoscope, spotting key moments to the very instant of the present."

"And that's how you knew about the safety-deposit box?" said Foster.

"And every other important fact. Now what do you suppose would happen if we let news of a home chronoscope get out? People might start out by watching their youth, their parents and so on, but it wouldn't be long before they'd catch on to the possibilities. The housewife will forget her poor, dead mother and take to watching her neighbor at home and her husband at the office. The businessman will watch his competitor; the employer his employee.

"There will be no such thing as privacy. The party line, the prying eye behind the curtain will be nothing compared to it. The video stars will be closely watched at all times by everyone. Every man his own peeping Tom, and there'll be no getting away from the watcher. Even darkness will be no escape because chronoscopy can be adjusted to the infrared, and human figures can be seen by their own body heat. The figures will be fuzzy, of course, and the surroundings will be dark, but that will make the titillation of it all the greater, perhaps. ... Hmp, the men in charge of the machine now experiment sometimes in spite of the regulations against it."

Nimmo seemed sick. "You can always forbid private manufacture—"

Araman turned on him fiercely. "You can, but do you expect it to do good? Can you legislate successfully against drinking, smoking, adultery or gossiping over the back fence? And this mixture of nosiness and prurience will have a worse grip on humanity than any of those. Good Lord, in a thousand years of trying we haven't even been able to wipe out the heroin traffic, and you talk about legislating against a device for watching anyone you please at any time you please that can be built in a home workshop."

Foster said suddenly, "I won't publish."

Potterley burst out, half in sobs, "None of us will talk. I regret—"

Nimmo broke in. "You said you didn't tab me on the chronoscope, Araman."

"No time," said Araman wearily. "Things don't move any faster on the chronoscope than in real life. You can't speed it up like the film in a book viewer. We spent a full twenty-four hours trying to catch the important moments during the last six months of Potterley and Foster. There was no time for anything else and it was enough."

"It wasn't," said Nimmo.

"What are you talking about?" There was a sudden infinite alarm on Araman's face.

"I told you my nephew, Jonas, had called me to say he had put important information in a safety-deposit box. He acted as though he were in trouble. He's my nephew. I had to try to get him off the spot. It took a while, then I came here to tell him what I had done. I told you when I got here, just after your man conked me that I had taken care of a few items."

"What? For Heaven's sake—"

"Just this: I sent the details of the portable chronoscope off to half a dozen of my regular publicity outlets."

Not a word. Not a sound. Not a breath. They were all past any demonstration.

"Don't stare like that," cried Nimmo. "Don't you see my point? I had popular publication rights. Jonas will admit that. I knew he couldn't publish scientifically in any legal way. I was sure he was planning to publish illegally and was preparing the safety-deposit box for that reason. I thought if I put through the details prematurely, all the responsibility would be mine. His career would be saved. And if I was deprived of my science-writing license as a result, my exclusive possession of the chronometric data would set me up for life. Jonas would be angry, I expected that, but I could explain the motive and we would split the take fifty-fifty ... Don't stare at me like that. How did I know—"

"Nobody knew anything," said Araman bitterly, "but you all just took it for granted that the government was stupidly bureaucratic, vicious, tyrannical, given to suppressing research for the hell of it. It never occurred to any of you that we were trying to protect mankind as best we could."

"Don't sit there talking," wailed Potterley. "Get the names of the people who were told—"

"Too late," said Nimmo, shrugging. "They've had better than a day. There's been time for the word to spread. My outfits will have called any number of physicists to check my data before going on with it and they'll call one another to pass on the news. Once scientists put neutrinics and pseudo-gravitics together, home chronoscopy becomes obvious. Before the week is out, five hundred people will know how to build a small chronoscope, and how will you catch them all?" His plum cheeks sagged. "I suppose there's no way of putting the mushroom cloud back into that nice shiny uranium sphere."

Araman stood up. "We'll try, Potterley, but I agree with Nimmo. It's too late. What kind of a world we'll have from now on I don't know, I can't tell, but the world we know has been destroyed completely. Until now, every custom, every habit, every tiniest way of life has always taken a certain amount of privacy for granted, but that's all gone now."

He saluted each of the three with elaborate formality.

"You have created a new world among the three of you. I congratulate you. Happy goldfish bowl to you, to me, to everyone, and may each of you fry in hell forever. Arrest rescinded."

Q5